ANDY GORDON.

CHAPTER I.

THE YOUNG JANITOR.

THE Hamilton Academy, under the charge of Rev. Dr. Euclid, stands on an eminence about ten rods back from the street, in the town of the same name. It is a two-story building, surmounted by a cupola, or belfry, and, being neatly painted brown and well cared for, is, on the whole, an ornament to the village.

It was a quarter of nine, when a boy of sixteen, rather showily dressed, ascended the academy hill and entered the front door, which was already open. He swung a small light cane in his hand—rather an unusual article for a schoolboy to carry—and it was clear, from his general appearance and bearing, that he had a high opinion of himself.

"I am early," he said to _____ "I shall

3

have a chance to look over my Latin before Dr. Euclid comes."

It may be supposed from this speech that Herbert Ross was an earnest student, but this would be altogether a mistake. The fact is, he had been playing with some companions till a late hour the previous evening, and this had prevented his paying the necessary attention to his lessons in Virgil.

As Dr. Euclid was strict in his requirements, and very slow to accept excuses, Herbert, to avoid trouble, wished to have, at any rate, a superficial acquaintance with the lesson.

As he entered the schoolroom he was met by a cloud of dust. A boy of about his own age was sweeping the floor. He had nearly completed his task, and was just about to sweep the pile of accumulated dust into the entry when Herbert Ross presented himself. The boy who was wielding the broom, the young janitor of the academy, being our hero, we may as well stop here and describe him.

His name was Andrew Gordon, commonly changed by his friends to Andy. He was a stout, well-made boy, with a face not exactly handsome, but bold, frank and good-humored; but about the mouth there were lines indicating firmness and resolution. He was evidently a boy who had a respect for himself.

It may be said, further, that Andy received his tuition free and a dollar a week for his services in taking care of the schoolhouse. He was the son of a widow, who was in receipt of a pension of twenty dollars a month from the government, as the widow of an officer who had surrendered his life during the Civil War on the field of Gettysburg. This, with what Andy could earn, was nearly all she and he had to live upon.

It may easily be supposed, therefore, that the dollar a week which Andy received from Dr. Euclid, or, rather, from the trustees of the academy, was an appreciable help in their frugal household.

Herbert Ross was the only son of the village lawyer, a man of private fortune, who lived in a style quite beyond the average mode of living among his neighbors. Herbert was impressed, as many boys are under such circumstances, with an idea of his consequence, and this made itself felt in his intercourse with his school fellows.

In particular he looked down upon Andy Gordon, the first in rank in his class, because he was poor and filled the position of school janitor, which he regarded as menial.

Andy knew very well how his proud classmate regarded him, but it did not materially diminish his happiness or cause him to lose even a minute's sleep.

"What are you kicking up such a dust for, Andrew Gordon?" asked Herbert, considerably ruffled in temper, for some of the dust had settled upon his clothing.

"I am sweeping the schoolroom, Herbert," said Andy, "as you see."

"You needn't cover me with your confounded dust," said Herbert, testily.

"I didn't see you coming in," said Andy, good-naturedly, "or I would have stopped a minute. The fact is, I am rather late this morning, or my job would be over."

"I'll give you a lesson to teach you to be more careful next time," said Herbert, who was getting more and more ill-natured, and, as is usual with young bullies, got more impudent on account of Andy's good nature.

As he spoke, he drew back his foot and kicked at the pile of dust which Andy had carefully swept to the doorway, spreading it over a considerable portion of the floor.

Good-humored as he was, Andy's eye grew stern, and his voice was quick and imperative, as he demanded:

"What did you do that for, Herbert Ross?"

"I told you already," said Herbert. "I am

a gentleman, and I don't mean to let a servant cover me with dust."

"I am the janitor of this academy," said Andy, "and if that is being a servant, then I am one. But there is one thing I tell you, Herbert. I won't allow any boy, gentleman or not, to interfere with my work."

"How can you help yourself?" asked Herbert, with a sneer.

"Take this broom and sweep up the pile of dust you have scattered," said the young janitor.

As he spoke he tendered the broom to Herbert.

"What do you mean?" demanded the young aristocrat, his dark face growing darker still with anger.

"I mean what I say," responded Andy, resolutely. "You must repair the mischief you have done."

"Must? You low-lived servant!" Herbert burst forth. "Do you know who you are talking to?"

This was rather ungrammatical, but it is a common mistake, and Herbert was too angry to think of grammar.

"I am talking to a boy who has done a mean action," retorted Andy. "Take that broom and sweep up the dust you have scattered."

Herbert by this time was at white heat. He seized the broom which was extended toward him, but instead of using it as he was requested, he brought it down upon Andy's shoulders.

It was not the handle, but the broom end which touched the young janitor, and he was not hurt; but it is needless to say that he considered himself insulted. Under such circumstances, though far from quarrelsome, it was his habit to act promptly, and he did so now.

First he wrested the broom from Herbert; then he seized that young gentleman around the waist, and, despite his struggles, deposited him forcibly on the floor, which was thick with dust.

" Two can play at your game, Herbert," he said.

" What do you mean? you low hound! " screamed Herbert, as he rose from the floor.

" I think you can tell, without any explanation," said Andy, calmly.

Herbert looked as if he would like to annihilate the young janitor, but there was something in the strong grasp which he had just felt which convinced him that Andy was stronger than himself, and he hesitated.

" Do you know that my father is one of the trustees of the academy? " he shouted, shaking his fist. "I'll get you discharged from your place."

"You can do what you like," answered Andy, "but you'd better get out of the way, for I'm going to sweep. I'll let you off from sweeping up, as you have had a lesson already."

"You'll let me off!" exclaimed Herbert, passionately. "You—a servant—give me a lesson! You don't know your place, you young beggar!"

"No more talk like that, Herbert Ross, for I won't stand it!" said Andy, firmly.

"I'll call you what I please!" retorted Herbert.

"If you call me another name, I'll lay you down in the dirt again!" said Andy.

Just then, at the open door, appeared the tall, dignified figure of Dr. Euclid, who was in time to hear the last words spoken.

"What's the matter, boys?" he asked, looking keenly from Andy to Herbert.

CHAPTER II.

HERBERT CONSIDERS HIMSELF INSULTED.

BOTH boys were surprised to see Dr. Euclid, for it was ten minutes before his usual hour of coming.

It happened, however, that he had had

occasion to go to the post office to deposit an important letter, and as it was so near the hour for commencing school, he had not thought it worth his while to go home again.

"What's the matter, boys?" repeated the doctor.

Herbert Ross, who was still fuming with anger, saw a chance to get the janitor into trouble, and answered, spitefully:

"That boy has insulted me!"

"How did he insult you?" inquired Dr. Euclid, rather surprised.

"He seized me, when I wasn't looking, and laid me down on the dirty floor!" exploded Herbert, looking at Andy as if he would like to wither him with a glance.

Dr. Euclid knew something of the character and disposition of Herbert, and reserved his judgment.

"What have you to say to this charge, Andrew?" he asked, mildly.

"It is true," said Andy—"all except my taking him unawares."

"What could induce you to make such an assault upon your fellow-student?" said the doctor.

In reply, Andy made a correct statement of the transaction, in mild and temperate language.

"Is this correct, Herbert?" asked the doctor. "Did you interfere with Andrew in the discharge of his duties?"

"I kicked the pile of dirt," Herbert admitted.

"Why did you do that?"

"Because I wanted to teach him a lesson."

"What lesson?"

"Not to cover a gentleman with dust when he entered the room," replied Herbert, in a pompous tone.

"By the word 'gentleman' you mean to designate yourself, I presume," said Dr. Euclid.

Herbert colored, for though the doctor's words were plain and unemphasized, they seemed to him to imply sarcasm.

"Certainly, sir," he answered.

"Those who claim to be gentlemen must behave as such," said Dr. Euclid, calmly. "It is clear that your being covered with dust was accidental, and you had no occasion to resent it."

"Had he any right to throw me down?" asked Herbert, biting his lips.

"Did you not strike him first?"

"Well, yes."

"Then it appears to me that you are quits. I don't approve of fighting, but I hold to the

right of self-defense. I don't think this affair
calls for any interference on my part," and the
doctor passed on to his desk.

Herbert Ross was very much mortified. He
had confidently expected that Andy would get
into trouble, and perhaps receive a punishment, certainly a reprimand, from the preceptor. As it was, he alone had incurred
censure.

He nodded his head viciously, reflecting:

"This isn't the last of it. The doctor is
partial to that young beggar, but the doctor isn't everybody. He's responsible to the
trustees, and my father is the most important
one. He'll find he's made a mistake."

Herbert was not at all improved in temper
by a sharp reprimand from the doctor, when
he came to recite his lesson, on the shabby
character of his recitation.

When recess came, he stalked up to Andy,
and said, menacingly:

"You look out, Andy Gordon! You'll get
into trouble before you know it!"

"Thank you for telling me!" said Andy,
calmly. "What sort of trouble will I get
into?"

"You think you're all right because Dr.
Euclid took your part this morning!" continued Herbert, not answering the question;

"but that isn't the end of the matter, by a long shot! The doctor isn't so great a man as he thinks he is."

"I never knew that he considered himself a great man," answered Andy.

"Well, he does. He doesn't know how to treat a gentleman."

"Why don't he?"

"He upholds you in what you did."

"He thinks it right to act in self-defense."

"He may have to act in self-defense himself. My father is one of the trustees of this academy."

"You said that this morning."

"He can turn the doctor out of office, and put in another teacher," continued Herbert.

"That isn't anything to me," said Andy. "Still, I have one thing to say."

"What is that?" asked Herbert, suspiciously.

"That he will have a big job on his hands when he undertakes it," said Andy.

"He can do it," repeated Herbert, jerking his head emphatically; "but he won't begin with that."

"Won't he?" said Andy, indifferently.

"No; he'll begin with you. I'm going to tell him to-night all that has happened, and he'll have you discharged. You can make up your mind to that."

If Herbert expected to see Andy exhibit fear or alarm, he was not gratified. Our hero, on the other hand, looked provokingly indifferent.

"Don't you think you could get me off, Herbert?" asked Andy, with a smile, which the young aristocrat did not quite understand.

"If you will beg my pardon before the boys for what you did," he said, magnanimously, "I won't do anything about it."

"That is very kind. I suppose you will be willing to ask my pardon first for striking me with the broom and calling me bad names."

"No, I won't. I only did and said what was proper."

"Then you won't get any apology out of me," returned Andy.

"You will lose your place, and have to leave school."

"I don't think I shall."

"My father will have you turned out, and another janitor appointed."

"The janitor is not appointed by the trustees. Dr. Euclid always appoints the janitor."

. This was news to Herbert. He had rather a vague idea of the powers of the trustees, and fancied that their authority extended to the appointment of so subordinate a person as the janitor.

"It doesn't make any difference," he declared, recovering himself. "The doctor will have to dismiss you, whether he wants to or not."

"You speak very positively," rejoined Andy, with a contemptuous smile, which Herbert resented.

"You'll find it's no laughing matter," said Herbert, hotly. "For a poor boy, you put on altogether too many airs."

Andy's manner changed.

"Herbert Ross," he said, "I've listened to your talk because it amused me, but I've heard enough of it. The only boy in school who puts on airs is yourself, and I, for one, don't mean to stand your impudence. Your father may be a very important person, but you are not. All your talk about Dr. Euclid's losing his place is ridiculous. You can go and talk to the doctor on the subject if you think it best."

Here Andy turned on his heel, and called out to Frank Cooper:

"Have a catch, Frank?"

"Yes, Andy."

The two boys began to throw a ball to each

other, by way of improving their practice, for both belonged to a baseball club, and Andy's special and favorite position was that of catcher.

"You seem to have considerable business with Herbert Ross," said Frank. "I thought we should have no time for practice."

Andy smiled.

"Herbert thinks he has business with me," he said.

"I shouldn't think it was very pleasant business, by the way he looks," said Frank.

Andy smiled, but said nothing.

None of the boys had been present when the little difficulty of the morning took place, and he thought it not worth mentioning.

When Herbert left school at the close of the afternoon session, he was fully resolved to make it hot for the young janitor, and for Dr. Euclid, whose censure he had again incurred for a faulty Greek recitation.

CHAPTER III.

DR. EUCLID RECEIVES A CALL.

DR. EUCLID lived in a comfortable dwelling-house not far from the Presbyterian Church. His family was small, consisting only of his wife and himself. Having no children, he devoted himself solely to the interests of the academy, of which he had been the principal for a space of fifteen years.

The doctor was an unusually learned man for the preceptor of an academy. He by no means confined his attention to the studies pursued in the institution, but devoted his leisure hours to reading classic authors, such as are read in our best colleges. He had published a carefully annotated edition of Greek tragedy, which had gained him a great deal of credit in the eyes of scholars. Indeed, he had received, only a short time previous, an invitation to the chair of Latin and Greek in a well-known college, and had been strongly tempted to accept, but had finally declined it, not being willing to leave the Hamilton Academy, to which he had become much attached, and his friends and neighbors in the village, by whom he was held in high esteem.

Dr. Euclid was seated in his library, examining a new classical book which had been sent him by the publishers, when the maid-servant opened the door, and said:

" Please, Dr. Euclid, there's a gentleman wants to see you."

" Do you know who it is, Mary? " asked the doctor, laying aside his book, with a look of regret.

"I think it's the lyyer man, sir."

"Oh, you mean the lawyer," said Dr. Euclid, smiling.

"That's what I said, sir."

"Well, show him up."

Almost immediately Brandon Ross, Esq., rather a pompous-looking individual, who tried to make himself look taller by brushing up his reddish hair till it stood up like a hedge above his forehead, entered the room.

"Good-evening, Mr. Ross!" said Dr. Euclid, politely.

He wondered why the lawyer had favored him with a call. It did not occur to him that it had any connection with the little difficulty of the morning between Herbert Ross and his young janitor.

"Ahem! Doctor, I am very well," said the lawyer.

"Take a seat, if you please."

"Thank you, sir. I can't stay long. I am occupied with some very important legal business just now."

Mr. Ross said this with an air of satisfaction. He always represented that he was occupied with important business.

"Then he won't stay long," thought the doctor. "Well, I am glad of that, for I want to get back to my book."

"You probably expected I would call," Squire Ross began.

"No; I can't say I did," answered the doctor, regarding his visitor with surprise.

"Surely, sir, after that outrageous assault upon my son this morning, an assault, sir, committed almost in your very presence, you could hardly suppose I, as Herbert's father, would remain calmly at home and ignore the affair?"

Mr. Ross said this in the tone in which he usually addressed juries, and he looked to see it produce an effect upon Dr. Euclid. But he was disappointed. An amused smile played over the face of the dignified scholar, as he answered:

"I certainly didn't connect your visit with the little matter you refer to."

"Little matter!" repeated the lawyer, indignantly. "Do I understand, Dr. Euclid, that you speak of a ruffianly assault upon my son Herbert as a little matter?"

Dr. Euclid wanted to laugh. He had a vivid sense of the ridiculous, and the lawyer's way of speaking seemed so disproportioned to the boyish quarrel to which he referred, that it seemed to him rather ludicrous.

"I was not aware, Mr. Ross, that such an

assault had been made upon your son," he replied.

"Surely you know, Dr. Euclid," said the
lawyer, warmly, "that your janitor, Andrew
Gordon, had assaulted Herbert?"

"I knew the boys had had a little difficulty," returned the doctor, quietly. "Your
son struck Andrew with a broom. Did he tell
you that?"

Mr. Ross was surprised, for Herbert had not
told him that.

"It was a proper return for the violent attack which the boy made upon him. I am glad
that my son showed proper resentment."

"I beg your pardon, Mr. Ross, but your son's
attack preceded Andrew's. It was Andrew
who acted in self-defense, or, if you choose to
call it so, in retaliation."

"I presume your account comes from
your janitor," said the lawyer, a little disconcerted.

"On the contrary, it comes from your son.
Herbert admitted to me this morning what I
have just stated to you."

"But," said Ross, after a pause, "Andrew
had previously covered him with dust, from
malicious motives."

"I deny the malicious motives," said the
doctor. "Your son entered the schoolroom

hurriedly, just as Andrew was sweeping out. Accidentally, his clothes were covered with dust."

" It suits you to consider it an accident," said the lawyer, rudely. " I view it in quite a different light. Your janitor is well known to be a rude, ill-mannered boy——"

" Stop there, Mr. Ross!" said Dr. Euclid, in a dignified tone. " I don't know where you got your information on this subject, but you are entirely mistaken. Andrew is neither rough nor ill-mannered. I considered him very gentlemanly, and, what I consider of quite as much importance, a thoroughly manly boy."

" Then, sir, I understand that you uphold him in his assault upon my son," said the lawyer, fiercely.

" I consider," said the doctor, in a dignified tone, " that he was entirely justified in what he did."

" Then, sir, allow me to say that I am utterly astounded to hear such sentiments from a man in your position. I do not propose to allow my son to be ill-treated by a boy so much his inferior."

" If you mean inferior in scholarship," said the doctor, " you are under a misapprehension. Andrew is in your son's class in Latin and

Greek, but he is quite superior to him in both of these languages."

This was far from agreeable information for the proud lawyer, though he could not help being aware that his son was not a good scholar.

" I referred to social position," he said, stiffly.

" Social position doesn't count for much in America," said Dr. Euclid, smiling. " Of course, Mr. Ross, you recall Pope's well-known lines :

" ' Honor and shame from no condition rise.
Act well your part—there all the honor lies.' "

" I don't agree with Pope, then. His lines are foolish. But I won't waste my time in arguing. I have come here this evening, Dr. Euclid, as one of the trustees of the Hamilton Academy, to insist upon Andrew Gordon's discharge from the position of janitor."

" I must decline to comply with your request, Mr. Ross. Andrew is a capable and efficient janitor, and I prefer to retain him."

" Dr. Euclid, you don't seem to remember that I am a trustee of the academy!" said the lawyer, pompously.

" Oh, yes, I do! But the trustees have nothing to do with the appointment of a janitor."

" You will admit, sir, that they have something to do with the appointment of a principal," said Brandon Ross, significantly.

"Oh, yes!" answered the doctor, smiling.

"And that it is wise for the principal to consult the wishes of those trustees."

"I presume I understand you, Mr. Ross," said Dr. Euclid, in a dignified tone, "and I have to reply that you are only one out of six trustees, and, furthermore, that as long as I retain the position which I have held for fifteen years, I shall preserve my independence as a man."

"Very well, sir! very well, sir!" exclaimed the lawyer, intensely mortified at the ignominious failure of his trump card, as he had regarded it. "I shall be under the necessity of withdrawing my son from the academy, since he cannot otherwise be secure from such outrages as that of this morning."

"If your son will respect the rights of others, he will stand in no danger of having his own violated. As to withdrawing him from school, you must do as you please. Such a step will injure him much more than any one else."

"I am the best judge of that!" said the lawyer, stiffly. "Good-evening, sir!"

"Good-evening!"

The troublesome visitor went out, and with a sigh of relief, Dr. Euclid returned to his book.

CHAPTER IV.

TROUBLE PREPARING FOR ANDY.

WHEN Lawyer Ross returned to his showy dwelling, he found Herbert eagerly waiting to hear an account of his mission.

Herbert was firmly of the opinion that his father and himself were the two most import- ant persons in Hamilton, and he confidently anticipated that Dr. Euclid would be over- awed by his father's visit, and meekly accede to his demand. He thought, with a pleasant sense of triumph, how it would be in his power to " crow over" the janitor, who had so audaciously ventured to lay a finger upon his sacred person.

He looked up eagerly when his father entered the room.

" Well, father, did you see Dr. Euclid? " he asked.

" Yes," replied the lawyer, in a tone by no means pleasant.

" Did he agree to discharge Andy Gordon? "

" No, he didn't."

Herbert looked perplexed.

" Did you ask him to? "

" Yes."

" Then I don't understand."

"There are a good many things you don't understand," said his father, giving a kick to the unoffending cat which lay on the rug before the fire, and forcing the astonished animal to vacate her comfortable quarters.

"I should think," Herbert ventured to say, "that Dr. Euclid wouldn't dare to disobey you, as you are a trustee."

"Dr. Euclid is an obstinate fool!" exploded the lawyer.

"It would serve him right if you kicked him out and appointed a new principal," insinuated Herbert.

Mr. Ross felt in the mood to do as his son advised, but he felt very doubtful of his ability to accomplish the displacement of so popular and highly esteemed a teacher. He was pretty sure that he could not talk over the other trustees to agree to so decided a step, but he was unwilling to confess it, even to his son. Therefore he spoke diplomatically.

"I cannot tell what I may do," he said. "It will depend upon circumstances. All I can say is that Dr. Euclid will sooner or later be sorry for upholding Andrew Gordon in his lawless acts."

"Does he uphold him?"

"Yes. He says that Andrew was perfectly justified in what he did."

" He ought to be ashamed of himself!" said Herbert, provoked.

" He says," continued Mr. Ross, who took a perverse pleasure in mortifying his son, as he had himself been mortified, " that Andrew is your superior."

" My superior!" exclaimed Herbert, more than ever exasperated. " That young beggar my superior!"

" He says Andrew is a better scholar than you!"

" Then I don't want to go to his confounded school any more. He doesn't seem to know how to treat a gentleman."

" You needn't go, Herbert, if you don't care to," said his father, more mildly.

" May I leave the academy? " asked Herbert, eagerly.

" Yes. After the course which Dr. Euclid has seen fit to adopt, I shall not force a son of mine to remain under his instruction. I told him so this evening."

" What did he say to that? " queried Herbert, who could not help thinking that Dr. Euclid would be very sorry to lose a pupil of his social importance.

" He didn't say much," said the lawyer, who was not disposed to repeat what the doctor actually did say.

" Then," said Herbert, " there is no use for me to study my Latin lesson for to-morrow."

" You may omit it this evening, but of course I cannot have you give up study. I may obtain a private tutor for you, or send you to some school out of town."

The lawyer hoped that this step, though personally inconvenient, and much more expensive, might injure Dr. Euclid by implying that one of the trustees lacked confidence in him as a teacher.

Herbert left the room, well pleased on the whole with the upshot of the affair.

Half an hour later an old man, Joshua Starr by name, was ushered into the lawyer's presence. He was a man bordering upon seventy, with pinched and wizened features, which bore the stamp of meanness plainly stamped upon them. By one method and another he had managed to scrape together a considerable property, not wholly in a creditable manner.

He had cheated his own brother out of three thousand dollars, but in a way that did not make him amenable to the law. He had lent money to his neighbors on usurious terms, showing no mercy when they were unable to make payment. Such was the man who came to the squire for help.

" Good-evening, Squire Ross!" he said.

" I've come to you on a little matter of business."

" Well, Mr. Starr, state your case."

" I've got a note agin' a party in town, which I want you to collect."

" Who is the party, Mr. Starr?"

" Waal, it's the Widder Gordon."

Squire Ross pricked up his ears.

" Go on," he said, beginning to feel interested.

" You see, I've got a note agin' her husband for a hundred dollars, with interest."

" But her husband is dead."

" Jes' so, jes' so! But he borrowed the money when he was alive, in the year 1862."

" And now it is 1866."

" Jes, so! You see it isn't outlawed. The note is good."

" Show me the note."

The lawyer took and scanned it carefully.

" It was to run for three months," he said.

" Jes' so!"

" Why didn't you present it for payment?"

" I did," said Starr. " But it wan't convenient for him to pay it."

" You don't usually give so much time to your creditors, Mr. Starr," said the lawyer, keenly.

" I didn't want to be hard on him," whined Starr.

"There's something under this," the lawyer thought.

"Have you presented it for payment to the widow?" asked Ross.

"Yes; and what do you think? She says her husband paid it. It's ridikilus!"

"In that case you would have surrendered the note or given a receipt."

"Jes' so, jes' so!" said Mr. Starr, eagerly. "You understand the case, square. Let her show the receipt, as I've got the note."

"How does she explain your having the note?"

"She says I had mislaid the note, and her husband agreed to take a receipt instead."

"But she don't show the receipt."

"No; that's where I've got her," chuckled the old man. "I say, square, ain't my claim good?"

"Certainly, if she can't show any receipt from you."

"Then you can collect it for me?"

"I can try; but I don't suppose she has any property."

"There's her furnitoor," suggested the old man.

"Well, you may leave the note, and I will see what I can do. Good-night!"

"Good-night, square!"

When the lawyer was left alone, there was a look of malicious satisfaction on his face.

"Now, Master Andrew Gordon," he said to himself, "I think I can make you rue the day when you assaulted my son. But for that, I wouldn't have meddled in this business, for Starr is an old rascal; but now it suits me to do it. The Widow Gordon and her precious son shall hear from me to-morrow!"

CHAPTER V.

A MESSENGER OF BAD TIDINGS.

THE next day was Friday—the last day of the school week. Andy went to school as usual, wondering how Herbert would treat him after their little difficulty of the day before; not that he cared particularly, but he felt some curiosity on the subject.

But Herbert was absent. We know that his father had agreed to take him away from school, but this was not suspected by Andy, nor, indeed, by Dr. Euclid, notwithstanding the threat of Mr. Ross.

The doctor could hardly believe the lawyer would be so foolish as to deprive his son of school privileges merely on account of a boyish difficulty with one of his fellow students.

Herbert was often absent for a single day.

Sometimes he had a convenient headache in the morning, when he felt indisposed to go, and neither his father nor mother interfered with him on such occasions.

Mr. Ross left his son quite independent, as long as Herbert did not contravene his own plans, and Mrs. Ross was foolishly indulgent.

"I suppose Herbert is sulking at home," thought Andy. "Well, he can do it, if he wants to. I shan't allow him to interfere with my work, even if he is a rich man's son and I am only a janitor."

Andy felt gartified at Dr. Euclid's evident approval of his conduct. The principal was strict, but just, and thus gained the respect of all his students.

There is nothing boys more strongly resent than injustice and undeserved reproof, and no teacher who expects to retain his influence will permit himself to indulge in either.

It is hardly necessary to say that Squire Ross had communicated to Herbert the business which Mr. Starr had intrusted to him, and that Herbert was very much pleased to hear it.

"That's good!" he said, emphatically. "Won't you let me go with you when you call on the Gordons?"

" No, Herbert. I can't do that."

" What harm will it do?" pleaded Herbert, disappointed.

" It wouldn't look well, and the neighbors would be sure to criticise."

" It won't make any difference if they do. You are a rich man, and can laugh at them."

" Still, I don't want to become unpopular. I think of running for office by and by. I stand a good chance of being nominated for State senator next fall, and it won't do to give people a chance to talk against me."

" Why don't you run for member of Congress, pa? "

" So I may, in good time. The State senatorship would be a good stepping-stone to it."

" When are you going to call on Mrs. Gordon? "

" To-night, probably."

" I hope Andrew will be at home. It will make him feel blue."

Herbert carefully abstained from calling our hero Andy, as everyone else did. He was afraid this familiarity would be interpreted into an admission of his social equality, and this he was far from being willing to concede.

When Herbert stayed home from school on

an ordinary week day, he found it rather hard to pass the time, having no companions to play with, and not being especially fond of reading.

It struck him that it might be a very good idea to be sauntering along the road between the academy and the Widow Gordon's, and, intercepting Andy, give him a hint that something disagreeable awaited him.

He proceeded to carry this plan into effect, and so it happened that Andy encountered Herbert, as he supposed, by accident.

Now Andy was not a boy to bear malice, and he accordingly accosted Herbert in his usual pleasant tone.

" Why weren't you at school to-day, Herbert? " he asked.   " Were you sick? "

" No, I'm well enough," answered the young aristocrat.

" Got up late, I suppose? " said Andy.

" No, I didn't.   I don't think I shall go to the academy any more."

" Why not? " inquired Andy, considerably surprised.

" Dr. Euclid's an old fogy."

" Dr. Euclid is an excellent teacher," said Andy, warmly.

" He don't know how to treat a gentleman," said Herbert.

" How do you make that out? "

" I'll tell you. He ought to have given you a thrashing for insulting me," said Herbert, darting a look of anger and hostility at his schoolfellow.

" Oh, that's what you mean! " said Andy, laughing. " I don't think that would be treating a gentleman properly."

" Do you mean yourself? " demanded Herbert.

" Of course."

" Do you call yourself a gentleman? "

This was asked with such insulting emphasis that Andy, good-natured as he was, flushed with indignation.

Still he answered, calmly:

" I mean to behave like a gentleman, and, as long as I do that, I call myself one."

Herbert laughed scornfully.

" Perhaps when you are living in the poorhouse you will call yourself a gentleman," he said.

" What have I got to do with the poorhouse? " Andy asked, looking Herbert steadily in the eye.

" I refer you to my father," said Herbert, mockingly:

" Explain yourself, or perhaps I may not treat you like a gentleman," said Andy, in a

tone which caused Herbert to draw back in-
voluntarily.

"My father has gone to see your mother on
business," said Herbert. "If you care to know
what sort of business, you had better go home
and find out."

Andy was taken by surprise. He could not
conceive what business the lawyer could have
with his mother, but he was oppressed by a
presentiment of evil. He left Herbert and hurried home.

CHAPTER VI.

A LAWYER'S VISIT.

MRS. GORDON was sitting at her sewing ma-
chine when a knock was heard at her humble
door.

She kept no servant, and, as usual, answered
the knock in person.

"Mr. Ross!" she said, in surprise, as she
recognized in her caller the wealthy village
lawyer.

"Yes, Mrs. Gordon," said Mr. Ross, blandly,
for he had determined in this business to figure
simply as the agent of another and carefully
to conceal that he felt any personal interest
in an affair which was likely to give the poor
widow considerable trouble. "Yes, Mrs. Gordon. I call upon a little matter of business."

"Won't you come in?" said the widow, not forgetting her politeness in her surprise.

"I believe I will trespass on your hospitality for a brief space," said the lawyer. "Are you quite well?"

"Thank you, sir—quite so." And she led the way into the little sitting-room. "Take the rocking-chair, Mr. Ross," said the widow, pointing to the best chair which the plainly furnished apartment contained.

"You are very kind," said the lawyer, seating himself gingerly in the chair referred to.

"Your son is at school, I suppose?" continued the lawyer.

"Yes, sir. It is nearly time for Andy to be home." And the mother's voice showed something of the pride she felt in her boy. "I believe your son is in his class, Mr. Ross."

"Yes, very likely," responded the lawyer, indifferently.

"You said you came on business?" inquired the widow.

"Yes, Mrs. Gordon. I fear the business may prove unpleasant for you, but you will remember that I am only an agent in the matter."

"Unpleasant!" repeated Mrs. Gordon, apprehensively.

"Yes. Mr. Joshua Starr has placed in my

hands, for collection, a note for one hundred dollars, executed by your late husband. With arrears of interest, it will amount to one hundred and thirty dollars, or thereabouts. I suppose you know something about it."

"Yes, Mr. Ross, I do know something about it. The note was paid by my husband during his life—in fact, just before he set out for the war—and Mr. Starr knows it perfectly well."

"You surprise me, Mrs. Gordon," said the lawyer, raising his eyebrows.

In fact, he was not at all surprised, knowing that Starr was an unprincipled man and not too honest to take advantage of any loss or omission on the part of his debtor.

"Didn't Mr. Starr say that we disputed his claim?" asked the widow.

"The fact is, Mrs. Gordon, I had very little conversation with Mr. Starr on the subject. He called at my house last evening and put the note into my hand for collection. I believe he said you had refused to pay it, or something of the kind."

"I refused to pay what had been paid already," said Mrs. Gordon, indignantly. "I regard Mr. Starr as a swindler."

"Softly, Mrs. Gordon! You must be cautious how you speak of an old and respected citizen."

"He may be old," admitted the widow; "but I deny that he is respected."

"Well, that is a matter of opinion," said the lawyer, diplomatically. "Meanwhile, he has the law on his side."

"How do you make that out, sir?"

"I have in my hands the note signed by your husband. If he paid it, why was it not given up?"

"I will tell you, sir. My husband was not a suspicious man, and he had confidence in others, crediting them with as much honesty as he himself possessed. When the note came due, he paid it; but Mr. Starr pretended that he had mislaid the note and couldn't lay hands on it. He told my husband he would give him a receipt for the money, and that would be all the same. He was laying a trap for him all the time."

"I don't see that. The proposal was perfectly regular."

"He thought, in case my husband lost the receipt, he would have the note and could demand payment over again. Oh, it was a rascally plot!"

"But," said the lawyer, "I suppose you have the receipt, and, in that case, you have only to show it."

"I am sorry to say that I have not been able

to find it anywhere. I have hunted high and low, and I am afraid my poor husband must have carried it away in his wallet when he went South with his regiment. The note was paid only the day before he left, out of the bounty money he received from the State."

"That would certainly be unfortunate," said Lawyer Ross, veiling the satisfaction he felt, "for you will, in that case, have to pay the money over again."

"Can the law be so unjust?" asked Mrs. Gordon, in dismay.

"You cannot call it unjust. As you cannot prove the payment of the money, you will have to bear the consequences."

"But I have no money. I cannot pay!"

"You have your pension," said the lawyer. "You can pay out of that. My client may be willing to accept quarterly installments."

"I need all I have for the support of Andy and myself."

"Then I am afraid—I am really afraid—my client will levy upon your furniture."

"Oh, heavens!" exclaimed the poor woman, in agitation. "Can such things be allowed in a civilized country?"

"I don't think you look upon the affair in the right light, Mrs. Gordon," said Lawyer Ross, rising from the rocking-chair in which he had been seated. "It is a common thing, and quite regular, I can assure you. I will venture to give you a week to find the receipt, though not authorized by my client to do so. Good-afternoon!"

As he was going out he met, on the thresh-hold, Andy, excited and out of breath.

The boy just caught a glimpse of his mother in tears, through the open door of the sitting room, and said to Mr. Ross, whom he judged to be responsible for his mother's grief:

"What have you been saying to my mother, to make her cry?"

"Stand aside, boy! It's none of your business," said the lawyer, who lost all his blandness when he saw the boy who had assaulted his son.

"My mother's business is mine," said Andy, firmly.

"You will have enough to do to attend to your own affairs," said the lawyer, with a sneer. "You made a great mistake when you made a brutal assault upon my son."

"And you have come to revenge yourself upon my mother?" demanded Andy, in a tone indicating so much scorn that the lawyer, case-hardened as he was, couldn't help winding.

"You are mistaken," he said, remembering

his determination to appear only as agent. " I came on business of my client, Mr. Starr. I shall take a future opportunity to settle with you."

He walked away, and Andy entered the cottage to learn from his mother what had passed between her and the lawyer.

This was soon communicated, and gave our hero considerable anxiety, for he felt that Mr. Starr, though his claim was a dishonest one, might nevertheless be able to enforce it.

" How did Mr. Ross treat you, mother? " he asked, fearing that the lawyer might have made his errand unnecessarily unpleasant.

CHAPTER VII.

THE LOST RECEIPT.

" Mr. Ross was very polite, Andy," said Mrs. Gordon.

" Then he didn't say anything rude or insulting? "

" No; far from it. He was very pleasant. He is acting only as the agent of Mr. Starr."

Andy was puzzled.

" Did he say anything about a quarrel between his son Herbert and myself? " he inquired.

"Not a word. I didn't know there had been one."

Thereupon Andy told the story with which we are already familiar.

"I thought he had come about that," he said.

"I wish he had. It wouldn't give us as much trouble as this note. He says we will have to pay it if we can't find the receipt."

"I wish old Starr was choked with one of his own turnips," said Andy, indignantly.

"Don't speak so, Andy!"

"I mean it, mother. Why, the old swindler knows that the note has been paid, but he means to get a second payment because we can't prove that it has been paid once."

"It is very dishonorable, Andy, I admit."

"Dishonorable! I should say it was. He knows that we are poor, and have nothing except your pension, while he is rich. He was too mean to marry, and has no one to leave his money to, and he can't live many years."

"That is all true, Andy."

"I would like to disappoint the old skin-flint."

"The only way is to find the receipt, and I am afraid we can't do that."

"I'll hunt all the evening," said Andy, resolutely. "It may come to light somewhere."

"I have hunted everywhere that I could

think of, and I am afraid it must be as I have long thought, that your poor father carried it away with him when he left for the army."

"If that is the case," said Andy, seriously, "we can never find it."

"No; in that case Mr. Starr has us at his mercy."

"What can we do?"

"Mr. Ross says he may agree to receive payment by installments from my pension."

"He shan't get a cent of your pension, mother!" said Andy, indignantly.

"Or else," continued the widow, "he may levy on our furniture."

"Did Mr. Ross say that?" asked Andy.

"Yes."

"I begin to think," thought Andy, "that Mr. Ross himself is interested in this matter. In spite of what he says, I believe he means to punish us for what passed between Herbert and myself."

If this was the case, Andy felt that matters were getting serious. All the more diligently he hunted for the lost receipt, leaving not a nook or cranny of the little cottage unexplored, but his search was in vain. The receipt could not be found.

"Mother," said he, as he took the candle to go to bed, "there's only one thing left to do.

To-morrow is Saturday, and I shan't need to go to school. I'll call on Mr. Starr, and see if I can't shame him into giving up his claim on us."

"There's no hope of that," said Mrs. Gordon. "You don't know the man."

"Yes, I do! I know he is a mean skinflint, but I can't do any worse than fail. I will try it."

CHAPTER VIII.

MR. STARR'S INVOLUNTARY RIDE.

THE farmhouse of Mr. Joshua Starr was situated about a mile from the village. It was a dilapidated old building, standing very much in need of paint and repairs, but the owner felt too poor to provide either.

Mr. Starr had never married. From early manhood to the age of sixty-nine he had lived in the same old house, using the same furniture, part of the time cooking for himself.

At one time he employed a young girl of fourteen, whom he had taken from the poorhouse to do his household work. She was not an accomplished cook, but that was unnecessary, for Mr. Starr had never desired a liberal table. She could cook well enough to suit him, but he finally dismissed her for two reasons. First, he begrudged paying her

seventy-five cents a week, which he had agreed
with the selectmen to do, in order to give the
girl the means of supplying herself with decent
clothes; and, secondly, he was appalled by her
appetite, which, though no greater than might
be expected of a growing girl, seemed to him
enormous.

At the time of which we speak, Mr. Starr
was living alone. He had to employ some help
outside, but in the house he took care of
himself.

It was certainly a miserable way of living
for a man who, besides his farm, had accumulated, by dint of meanness, not far from ten
thousand dollars, in money and securities,
and owned his farm clear, in addition.

Andy went up to the front door, and used
the old brass knocker vigorously, but there was
no response.

"I suppose Mr. Starr is somewhere about
the place," he said to himself, and bent his
steps toward the barn.

There he found the man of whom he was in
search.

Joshua Starr was attired in a much-patched
suit, which might have been new thirty years
before. Certainly he did not set the rising
generation a wasteful example in the matter
of dress.

The old man espied Andy just before he got within hearing distance, and guessed his errand.

"Howdy do, Andy Gordon?" he said, in a quavering voice.

"All right!" answered Andy, coolly.

If it had been anyone else, he would have added, "thank you," but he did not feel like being ordinarily polite to the man who was conspiring to defraud his mother.

"I'm tollable myself," said Joshua, though Andy had not inquired. "The rheumatiz catches me sometimes and hurts me a sight."

"You ought to expect it at your age," said Andy.

"I ain't so very old," said Mr. Starr, uneasily.

"How old are you?"

"Sixty-nine."

"That seems pretty old to me."

"My father lived to be nigh on to eighty," said Joshua. "He wa'n't no healthier than I be, as I know of."

"You might live to be as old, if you would eat nourishing food."

"So I do! Who says I don't?"

"Nancy Gray, the girl that worked for you, says you didn't allow yourself enough to eat."

"That girl!" groaned the old man. "It's well I got red on her, or she'd have eaten me out of house and home. She eat three times as much as I did, and I'm a hardworking man and need more than she does."

"I suppose you know what I've come to speak to you about, Mr. Starr," said Andy, thinking it time to come to business.

"Have you come to pay that note I hold agin' your mother?" asked the old man, with suppressed eagerness.

"My mother owes you nothing," said Andy, firmly.

"You're mistaken, Andy. She owes me a hundred dollars and interest, and I've got the dockyment to prove it."

"You know very well, Mr. Starr, that my father paid you that money long ago."

"When did he pay it?"

"Just before he started for the war. You needn't ask, for you know better than I do."

"Yes, I do know better'n you do," said the old man. "Ef he paid it, why didn't he get the note? I'd like to know that, Andy Gordon."

"That's easily answered. It was because you pretended you had mislaid it, and you asked him to take a receipt instead."

"That ain't a very likely story, Andy. Still,

ef you've got the receipt to show, it may make a difference."

"We haven't been able to find the receipt," said Andy.

"Of course you ain't, and a good reason why. There never was any receipt. You don't expect I'd give a receipt when the note wasn't paid."

"No, I don't; but we both know the note was paid."

"Then, all I can say is you was mighty shif-'less to lose it," said the old man, chuckling.

"An honorable man wouldn't take advantage of such a loss, Mr. Starr. He wouldn't be willing to defraud a poor widow, even if he had the power to do it."

"You're wandering from the p'int, Andrew. Ef the money was paid, you can show the receipt, and then I won't have another word to say."

"I am afraid my father must have taken the receipt with him when he went to the war."

"Jes' so—jes' so!" chuckled Mr. Starr, his chuckle bringing on a fit of coughing.

"What do you mean to do?" asked Andy, a little anxiously.

"Waal, I want to collect my money. A hundred dollars is a good deal of money. I can't afford to lose it."

"We don't owe it."

"The law says you do."

"At any rate, we can't pay it. We have no money."

"Ain't your mother got her pension, Andrew?"

"Yes, she has, and she will keep it! Not a cent will you get out of it!"

"Then I'll have to take your furniture," said Mr. Starr, placidly.

"I believe you are the meanest man in town!" said Andy, indignantly.

"I want my own property," said the old man, doggedly, "and you may tell your mother so."

While the two had been conversing, the old man, shovel in hand, had led the way into the barnyard, where there were three cows.

One of them, unseen by Mr. Starr, being out of humor, probably, lowered her head and, approaching the old man from behind, fairly lifted him up to a sitting position on her head. Mechanically he grasped her horns, and in this position was carried rapidly round the yard, much to his own dismay and Andy's amusement.

"Take her off, Andy!" exclaimed the frightened and bewildered old man. "She'll kill me!"

"If I touch her, she'll throw you on the ground," said Andy, between paroxysms of laughter.

"Do somethin' to help me, or I'm a dead man!" shrieked Joshua, clinging tighter to the cow's horns. "If you'll help me, I'll take off a dollar from the note."

Andy knew that the old man was in no real danger, and stood still, while the triumphant cow ran about the yard with her terrified master between her horns.

"Oh, dear! Will nobody help me?" howled Joshua. "Is the cow crazy?"

"I think she must be, Mr. Starr," said Andy, gravely.

"I shall be killed, and I'm only sixty-nine!" wailed the old man, who by this time had lost his hat.

"Shall I shoot her?" asked Andy, displaying a toy pistol, which was quite harmless.

"No, don't!" exclaimed the old man, turning pale. "You might hit me! Besides, I gave thirty dollars for her. Oh, I never expected to die this way," he added, dismally.

But the cow was by this time tired of her burden, and, with a jerk of her head, dislodged her proprietor, who fell prostrate in a pile of manure.

Andy ran to pick him up, and helped him into the house.

" Do you think any of my bones is broken? " asked Joshua, anxiously.

" I don't see how they can be. You fell in a soft place," said Andy, wanting to laugh.

" I'll sell that cow as quick as I get a chance," said Joshua. " Don't you tell any-body what's happened, or you may spile the sale."

Andy tried to introduce the subject of the note again, but Joshua was too full of the acci-dent to talk about it. Finally, discouraged by his poor success, he went home.

On the way he met Louis Schick, a school-fellow, of German extraction, who hailed him.

" You'd better go to the post office, Andy. There's a big parcel there for your mother."

" A parcel? "

" Yes; it's too big for a letter."

Wondering what it could be, Andy went to the post office.

The parcel he found there was of great im-portance.

CHAPTER IX.

A GIFT FROM THE DEAD.

THE village post office was located in a drug store, and the druggist had plenty of time to attend to the duties of the office, as well as the calls of his regular customers.

Hamilton was so healthy a village that it hardly furnished a sufficient demand for drugs and medicines to support a man of the most moderate tastes. But, with the addition of his salary as postmaster, Mr. Bolus was able to maintain a small family in comfort.

" I suppose you want some pills, Andy? " said Mr. Bolus, as our hero entered the office.

" No, sir," answered Andy. " I hope I shan't want any of them for a long time to come. Louis Schick told me there was something in the office for mother."

" So there is—and a large parcel, too."

He went into the post-office corner and produced a large, thick parcel, wrapped in a long, yellow envelope.

" Here it is, Andy," said Mr. Bolus. " I hope it's something valuable."

Andy took the package and looked eagerly at the address.

His mother's name and address were on the envelope, and it seemed to be postmarked at some town in Pennsylvania.

" Do you know anybody in the place where the package comes from? " asked the postmaster.

" No," answered Andy. " That is, I don't— perhaps mother may. It feels like a wallet," added Andy, thoughtfully.

" So it does. I hope, for your mother's sake, the wallet is full of money."

" I am afraid there isn't much chance of that," replied Andy. " Well, I'll go home and carry it to mother."

Andy put the parcel in his inside coat pocket and took the nearest way home.

As he entered the house he did not immediately speak of the parcel, his thoughts being diverted by his mother's question:

" Well, Andy, did you see Mr. Starr? "

" Yes, mother, I saw him," answered Andy, soberly.

" Well, what does he say? " Mrs. Gordon inquired, anxiously.

" Nothing that's encouraging. Mother, I believe he is one of the meanest men I ever knew."

" He must know that your father paid that note."

" Of course he knows it. A man doesn't often forget such a thing as that. At any rate, Mr. Starr isn't that kind of man."

" What did he say when you told him the note had been paid? "

" That, of course, we could show the receipt."

" It was a cunningly laid plot," said Mrs. Gordon, indignantly. " He kept back the note,

in the hope that your father would mislay
the receipt.   Perhaps he was even wicked
enough to hope that he would be killed, and
so clear the way for carrying out his fraudulent scheme."

" I shouldn't wonder if it were so, mother.
I believe the old man would sell himself for
money."

Then, chancing to think of Mr. Starr's in-
voluntary ride on one of his own cows, Andy
began to laugh heartily, considerably to the
surprise of his mother.

" I can't see anything to laugh at, Andy,"
she said, wonderingly.

" You would have laughed if you had seen
what happened while I was talking to Mr.
Starr."

And Andy proceeded to give an account of
the scene.

Mrs. Gordon smiled, but she was too much
impressed by the serious position in which they
were placed to feel as much amusement as
Andy.

" I am afraid, Andy," she said, " that Mr.
Starr will deprive us of our furniture, unless
something unexpected turns up in our
favor."

This recalled to Andy's mind the packet
which he had just brought from the post
office.

" That reminds me, mother," he said, quickly. " I got a letter, or package, from the post office just now, for you. Perhaps there is something in it that may help us."

He drew from his pocket the package and handed it to his mother.

Mrs. Gordon received it with undisguised amazement.

" Erie, Pennsylvania," she read, looking at the postmark. " I don't know anybody there."

" Open it, mother. Here are the scissors."

Mrs. Gordon cut the string which helped confine the parcel, and then cut open the envelope.

" It is your father's wallet, Andy," she said, in a voice of strong emotion, removing the contents.

" Father's wallet? How can it be sent you from Erie at this late day? " asked Andy, in surprise equal to his mother's.

" Here is a note. Perhaps that will tell," said his mother, drawing from the envelope a folded sheet of note paper. " I will read it."

The note was as follows:

" DEAR MADAM: I have to apologize to you for retaining so long in my possession an article which properly belongs to you, and ought long ago to have been sent to you. Before explaining the delay, let me tell you how this wallet came into my possession.

"Like your lamented husband, I was a soldier in the late war. We belonged to different regiments and different States, but accident made us acquainted. Toward the close of a great battle I found him lying upon the ground, bleeding freely from a terrible wound in the breast. Though nearly gone, he recognized me, and he said, as his face brightened:

"'Ramsay, I believe I am dying. Will you do me a favor?'

"'You have only to ask,' I said, saddened by the thought that my friend was about to leave me.

"'You'll find a wallet in my pocket. Its contents are important to my family. Will you take it and send it to my wife?'

"Of course I agreed to do it, and your husband, I have reason to know, died with a burden lifted from his mind in that conviction. But before the action was over I, too, was stricken by one of the enemy's bullets. My wound was not a dangerous one, but it rendered me incapable of thought or action. I was sent to the hospital, and my personal effects were forwarded to my family.

"Well, in course of time I recovered, and, remembering your husband's commission, I searched for the wallet—but searched in vain. I feared it had been taken by some dishonest person. The war closed and I returned home. I ought to have written to you about the matter, but I feared to excite vain regrets. Perhaps I decided wrongly, but I resolved to say nothing about the wallet, since it seemed to be irretrievably lost.

"Yesterday, however, in examining an old trunk, I, to my great joy, discovered the long-missing wallet. I have taken the liberty to look into it, but cannot judge whether the contents, apart from the money, are of importance. My duty, however, is plain—to forward you the article at once. I do so, therefore, and beg you to relieve my anxiety by apprising me as soon as you receive it.

"Once more let me express my regret that there has been so great a delay, and permit me to subscribe myself your husband's friend,

"BENJAMIN RAMSAY."

It is needless to say that both Andy and his mother were deeply interested in a letter which threw light upon the closing scene in the life of one so dear to them.

"Andy," said his mother, "open the wallet. I cannot."

The sight of it naturally aroused painful recollections in the heart of the bereaved wife.

Andy was not slow in obeying his mother's directions.

The first, and most prominent in the list of contents, was a roll of greenbacks. The bills were of various denominations, and they aggregated the sum of forty-five dollars.

" Money saved by your poor father from his salary," said Mrs. Gordon.

" He will be glad that it has come into our hands, mother."

" Yes; he was always thinking of those he left behind."

" Here are some papers, too, mother," said Andy. " They seem to be receipted bills."

" I wish," sighed the widow, " that the receipt from Mr. Starr might be found among them."

One by one Andy opened the papers, hoping, but not much expecting, that the missing receipt might be found.

" Here it is, mother!" he exclaimed at last, triumphantly, flourishing a slip of paper.

" Let me see it, Andy," said his mother, hurriedly.

" Don't you see, mother? Here is his signature—Joshua Starr. I wonder what the old rascal will say to that?"

" The Lord has listened to my prayer, Andy. He has brought us out of our trouble."

" Don't say anything about it, mother," said Andy. " I want to see how far the old swindler will go. I wonder what he will say when we show him the receipt? "

CHAPTER X.

THE FATE OF A BULLY.

THE next day, Herbert Ross reappeared at school. As we know, it had been his intention not to go back unless Dr. Euclid would dismiss Andy from the post of janitor.

Now, however, he and his father saw a way of getting even with our hero, by the help of Mr. Starr, and the note which he had placed in the lawyer's hands for collection.

The prospect of distressing the family of his poor schoolmate was exceedingly pleasant to Herbert, who from time to time cast glances of triumph at Andy, which the latter well understood. But, with the means at hand to foil his ungenerous foe, Andy, too, could afford to be in good spirits, and his face showed that he was so.

This puzzled Herbert not a little. He had expected that Andy would be cast down, and was annoyed because he seemed so far from despondent.

" Of course they can't pay the note," thought

Herbert, with momentary apprehension.
"But of course they can't! I don't suppose
they have got ten dollars in the house. I mean
to go round when the sheriff seizes the furniture. Andy won't look quite so happy then,
I am thinking!"

Herbert recited his Latin lesson as poorly as
usual—perhaps even more so, for his mind had
been occupied with other things—and Dr.
Euclid, who never flattered or condoned the
shortcomings of a pupil on account of his
social position, sharply reprimanded him.

"Herbert Ross," he said, "how do you expect to get into college if you recite so dis-
gracefully?"

"The lesson was hard," said Herbert, coolly,
shrugging his shoulders.

"Hard, was it?" retorted the doctor.
"There are some of your classmates who succeeded in learning it. Andrew Gordon, did
you find the lesson very hard?"

"No, sir," answered Andy, promptly.

Herbert looked at his successful classmate
with a sneer.

"I can't expect to compete with a janitor!"
he said, slowly.

"Then," said the doctor, provoked, "the
sooner you obtain the position of a janitor the
better, if that is going to improve the character
of your recitations!"

"I wouldn't accept such a position!" said Herbert, coloring with anger.

"You are not likely to have one offered you," said the doctor. "A boy who neglects his lessons is not likely to discharge well the duties of any position."

Herbert bit his lips in annoyance, but he did not dare to say anything more, for he saw, by the ominous flashing of Dr. Euclid's eyes, that he was in no mood to suffer impertinence.

He began to regret that he had been induced to return to school. He felt that it was very reprehensible in Dr. Euclid to treat the son of his most important patron with so little deference, or, indeed, respect.

"But never mind!" thought Herbert. "I will soon have my revenge. Father has given Mrs. Gordon a week's grace, and then she will have to pay the note or lose her furniture."

Two days later an incident occurred which incensed Herbert still more against Andy, and, as usual, the fault was Herbert's.

The young aristocrat was a natural bully. Like most bullies he was deficient in courage, and preferred to cope with a boy smaller than himself. For this reason he was both hated and feared by the young boys of the village, as he seldom lost an opportunity to annoy and tease them.

On Saturday there was no session of the Hamilton Academy. Teacher and scholars enjoyed a season of rest which was welcome to both.

After getting through a late breakfast, Herbert Ross took his hat, and sauntered through the village in search of something to amuse him or while away his time. Though he was glad to stay at home from school, he found Saturday rather a dull day.

There was a young clerk with whom he used sometimes to play billiards in the evening, but during the day it was difficult to find anyone who was not employed.

" I wish father would move to New York or Philadelphia," thought Herbert, yawning. " Hamilton is a dull hole, and there's absolutely nothing to do. If we lived in a city, there wouldn't be any difficulty in finding company and enjoying myself."

There was a vacant field, unfenced, near the engine house, which was used as a sort of common by the village boys, and in the course of his walk Herbert Ross came to it.

Two boys of ten were playing marbles in one corner of the field. Their names were Harry Parker and John Grant.

" I'll have some fun with them," thought Herbert.

He stood watching the boys for a minute or two, then, stooping suddenly, seized the marbles with which they were playing.

"Give me those marbles, Herbert Ross," cried Johnny Grant.

"What'll you give to get them back?" asked Herbert.

"It's mean to break up our game," said Harry.

"Here, then, come and get them," said Herbert.

Harry approached, and extended his hand to receive the marbles, but Herbert, with a taunting laugh, drew back his own hands, and put them into his pocket.

Johnny had a spirit of his own, though he was a small boy, and he doubled up his small fists, and said, angrily:

"You have no business to keep our marbles."

"What are you going to do about it?" demanded Herbert, provokingly.

"I know what I'd do if I was as big as you," said Johnny, hotly.

"Well, what would you do, you little bantam?"

"I'd give you a licking and make you cry."

"Hear the small boy talk!" said Herbert, bursting into a laugh.

" It's because we are small boys that you interfere with us," said Harry. " You don't dare
to take one of your size."

" Look here, you little rascal, you are getting impudent," said Herbert, who was sensi-
tive to an imputation that he knew to be well
founded. " If you ain't careful, I'll do something worse than take your marbles."

" What will you do?" asked Johnny,
spiritedly.

" What will I do? Come here and I'll show
you."

Johnny, in no way frightened, approached,
and Herbert, seizing him by the collar, tripped
him up, depositing him upon the ground.

" That's the way I punish impudence," said
Herbert.

There had been a witness to his cowardly
act.

" What are you doing there, Herbert Ross?"
demanded Andy, who had just come up.

" None of your business!" retorted Herbert;
but he looked disturbed.

" Harry, what has he been doing to you?"
asked Andy.

Harry and Johnny both told their story.

Andy turned to Herbert, with eyes full of
contempt.

" You ought to be ashamed of yourself, Her-

bert Ross, to tease little boys. Give them back
their marbles."

" I will give them back when I get ready,"
said Herbert, doggedly.

" Give them up now, or you will be sorry for
it."

" Mind your business!" retorted Herbert,
and turned to walk away.

Before he well knew what was going to happen, the young bully found himself lying on
his back, in the very spot where he had deposited Johnny a minute before, with Andy
bending over him.

" Let me up, you brute!" he screamed.

" So I will, when you have given up the
marbles."

Herbert struggled, but in the end was
obliged to surrender the marbles.

As he rose from the ground he shook his fist
at Andy, and shouted, with passion:

" You'll repent this, Andrew Gordon! You'll
be a beggar inside of a week, and in State's
prison before the year's out!"

" Thank you for your good wishes!" said
Andy, coolly. " I'll take the risk of both."

As Herbert slunk home discomfited, he felt
that he hated Andy Gordon more than any one
in the world, and vowed to be revenged.

CHAPTER XI.

ANDY IS ENGAGED FOR POLICE DUTY.

" I WONDER how it is," said Andy to himself, as he walked home, " that I am always getting into a quarrel with Herbert Ross? I don't think it's my fault. I couldn't stand by and see those two little boys imposed upon without interfering. I suppose Herbert is angrier with me than ever, and that he will report this to his father, and get him to proceed against us at once. No matter; we shall be prepared to see him."

Andy was more than ever thankful that the all-important receipt was in his mother's possession. Whatever the lawyer might say, he believed that he was intending to punish them in the interest of his son.

In one respect, however, Andy made a mistake. Herbert did not report this last difficulty at home.

He was aware that he had not figured to advantage in his treatment of the two little boys, and any investigation of the matter would reveal this fact.

It would not be long now before he would have the satisfaction of seeing Andy and his mother in serious trouble, and, though impatient, he decided to wait for that. Then the triumph would be his.

When Andy reached home, he found that his mother had callers.

In a lonely situation, about a quarter of a mile beyond the farmhouse of Mr. Joshua Starr, lived two maiden ladies—Susan and Sally Peabody—both over fifty years of age.

Their father had died thirty years before, leaving them a cottage, with an acre of land, and some twelve thousand dollars in stocks and bonds.

Living economically, this sum had materially increased, and they were considered in the village rich ladies, as, indeed, they were, since their income amounted to more than twice their expenditures, and they were laying up probably five hundred dollars annually.

They were very good and kind, simple-hearted old ladies, and very much respected in the village.

The elder of these ladies, Miss Sally Peabody, Andy found in his mother's plain sitting-room.

As he entered, he heard Miss Peabody say:

"I should like to borrow your Andy to-night, Mrs. Gordon, if you have no objection."

Mrs. Gordon supposed that her visitor had

some work which she wished Andy to do, and as the latter was always glad of a job, she answered :

" I am sure, Miss Sally, that Andy will be glad to do anything that you require."

" I don't want him to do anything," answered Miss Peabody. " I want him to sleep at our house to-night."

Mrs. Gordon looked a little puzzled, but Miss Sally went on to explain.

" You see, Mrs. Gordon, we had a sum of five hundred dollars paid in unexpectedly this morning, and we can't get it to the bank till Monday. Now, it makes my sister nervous to think of having such a sum of money in the house. I was reading in the papers of a burglar entering a house at night in Thebes—the next village—and it might happen to us. I don't know what we should do, as we have no man in the house."

" Andy isn't a man," said Mrs. Gordon, smiling.

" No, he isn't a man, but he is a good stout boy, and we should feel safer if he were in the house."

" What an uncommonly sensible old lady Miss Peabody is ! " thought Andy.

He felt proud of his presence being supposed to be a safeguard against housebreakers.

"I'll go, Miss Peabody," he said, promptly.

"But, Andy," said his mother, "you could do no good."

"I don't know about that, mother," said Andy.

"You would be no match for a bold, bad man, and I don't like to think of your being in danger."

"Oh, you're a woman, mother, and don't understand!" answered Andy, good-humoredly. "I can scare a burglar away if he tries to get in."

"I don't suppose, really, that there is any danger of the house being entered," said Miss Peabody; "but still we shall feel safer with Andy in the house."

"Why don't you engage a man, Miss Sally?" asked the widow.

"The very man we engaged might rob us of the money."

"But you might engage some one whom you knew."

"Five hundred dollars would be a great temptation to one who was generally honest. No, Mrs. Gordon, I would much rather have Andy. If you will let him stay at our house to-night and to-morrow night, I will pay him for his trouble."

"Oh, I wouldn't ask anything for it, Miss Peabody!" said Andy.

"But I should insist on paying you all the same, Andy. My sister and I make it a rule never to ask a service of any one without paying for it. With our income as large as it is, we should think ourselves mean if we acted otherwise."

"You are very different from your neighbor, Mr. Starr," said Mrs. Gordon.

"I am really afraid that Mr. Starr is too fond of money," said Miss Sally, mildly. "I don't want to be too severe upon him, but I am afraid he is a little too close."

"A little too close!" replied Andy. "He is the meanest man I ever met."

"Are you not a little too severe, Andy?" asked the spinster.

"Not a bit. He is trying to make mother pay a note over twice."

"I can hardly believe such a thing."

"Then I will tell you all about it," said Andy, and he gave an account of the matter.

"And do you think you will have to pay it?" asked Miss Peabody, in a tone of sympathy.

Mrs. Gordon was about to explain why they would be spared the necessity, but a warning look from Andy prevented her.

Miss Peabody, with all her virtues, was fond

of talking, and Andy's plan of confounding his adversary would be spoiled.

"No, I don't think we shall have to pay it," Andy hastened to say. "We have a plan, but we don't like to speak of it just yet, for fear Mr. Starr will hear of it."

"If he really insists on his demand," said Miss Sally, "perhaps sister Susan and I can help you. How large is the note?"

"With interest it would amount to over a hundred dollars—perhaps thirty dollars more."

"We might advance the money, and you could give us a note."

"You are very kind, Miss Sally," said Mrs. Gordon, gratefully; and she paused and looked at Andy.

"We shall not pay it at all if we can help it, Miss Peabody," said Andy, "for we don't believe in rewarding Mr. Starr's dishonesty; but, if we find ourselves obliged to do so, we shall remember your kind offer."

"You are a true friend, Miss Sally," said the widow. "We could give no security, except our furniture. We might give you a bill of sale of that."

"As if I would take it, Mrs. Gordon! No, we have every confidence in your honesty, and even if you could not repay it, Andy would some day be able to."

"And I would do it, too, Miss Peabody,"
said Andy, stoutly. "But I don't believe we
shall need to ask you for the money."

"It would be a pity to have to pay the
note over again. I am really surprised at Mr.
Starr," said Miss Sally, who never used strong
language in commenting upon the moral de-
linquencies of her neighbors.

"When do you want Andy to come over?"
asked Mrs. Gordon.

"We should be glad to have him come to supper. It will seem pleasant to us to have company. Susan and I get tired sometimes of only
seeing one another's faces."

"Very well, Miss Peabody, I will be on
hand."

"I suppose there is no fear of your having
to fight burglars," said Mrs. Gordon. "No
burglary has been known here for years."

"No, I suppose not," answered Andy. "I
shan't have any chance to show off my bravery."

He might have come to a different opinion
if he had seen the villainous-looking tramp,
who, skulking near the house, had heard,
through the open window, the first and most
important part of the conversation.

CHAPTER XII.

MIKE HOGAN.

IN the summer season not a few of the desperate characters who, at other times, lurk in the lanes and alleys in our cities, start out on vagabond tramps through the country districts.

Mike Hogan was a fit representative of this class. He was a low-browed ruffian, with unkempt hair and a beard of a week's growth, with a look in his eyes that inspired distrust.

He was physically strong, and abundantly able to work, but preferred to dispense with labor, and live on the credulity or the fears of his fellow men.

Mike had served a term at Sing Sing, but punishment in no way altered his way of life. If anything, it confirmed him in his opposition to the law and his worthless habits.

He had been on the tramp now for two weeks, and accident had brought him to the neighborhood of Hamilton a couple of days before.

Mike had already made two calls, though he had only been an hour in the village. The first was to the house of Mr. Ross, the lawyer.

The master of the house was not at home, but Herbert was in the front yard. In fact, he was sitting on the doorstep, whittling.

Mike's experience taught him that children are generally less suspicious, and more easily moved to compassion, than their elders.

He therefore addressed himself with some confidence to Herbert, of whose disposition he knew nothing, or he would not have expected any help from him or through his influence.

" Young gentleman," he said, in a whining voice, as he rested his elbows on the top of the front gate, " I am a poor man——"

Herbert looked up, and surveyed the uncouth visitor with profound disdain. He always despised the poor, and made little discrimination between the deserving and the undeserving.

" You don't look very rich," he said, after a pause.

His tone was not particularly compassionate, but Mike did not detect the nature of his feelings.

" Indeed, young sir," he continued, in the same whining tone, " I have been very unfortunate."

" You have seen better days, I suppose," said Herbert, who had not the slightest idea of giving Hogan anything, but meant to play

with him as a cat does with a mouse before
sending him away.

"Yes, I have," said Hogan. "Once I was
prosperous, but ill health and misfortune came,
and swept away all my money, and now I have
to travel around and ask a few pennies of
kind strangers."

"Why don't you go to work? You look
strong enough," said Herbert.

And in this he was perfectly right.

"Why don't I work? I ain't able," answered the tramp.

"You look strong enough."

"You shouldn't judge by looks, young gentleman. I have fever 'n' ager awful, and the
rheumatism is in all my joints. You look rich
and generous. Can't you spare a few pennies
for a poor man?"

"You mustn't judge by looks," said Herbert,
laughing at his own repartee. "My father's
rich, but he don't give anything to tramps."

Now the professional tramp, although quite
aware of his own character, objects to being
called a tramp. He does not care to see himself as others see him.

Mike Hogan answered shortly, and without his customary whine:

"I am not a tramp. I'm an honest, poor
man."

"Honest!" repeated Herbert. "I shouldn't wonder if you had just come out of State's prison."

This remark Mike Hogan considered altogether too personal. The fact that it was true made it still more offensive. His tone completely changed now, and, instead of a whine, it became a growl, as he retorted:

"You'd better keep your tongue between your teeth, young whipper-snapper! You can't insult me because I am a poor man."

"You'd better look out," said Herbert, angrily. "My father's a lawyer, and a justice of the peace, and he'll have you put in the lock-up."

"Come out here, and I'll wring your neck, you young villain!" said Mike Hogan, whose evil temper was now fully aroused.

"I wish father was here," said Herbert, indignantly.

"I'd lick you both, and make nothing of it!" exclaimed the tramp.

"I thought you were not strong enough to work," sneered Herbert.

"I am strong enough to give you a beating," growled Hogan.

"Go away from here! You have no business to lean on our gate!"

"I shall lean on it as long as I please!"

said the tramp, defiantly. " Are you coming out here? "

If Mike Hogan had been a small boy, Herbert would not have been slow in accepting this invitation, but there was something in the sinister look and the strong, vigorous frame of Mike Hogan which taught him a lesson of prudence.

Herbert had never before wished so earnestly that he were strong and muscular. It would have done him good to seize the intruder, and make him bellow for mercy, but his wish was fruitless, and Mike remained master of the situation.

At this moment, however, he was re-enforced by his dog, Prince, who came round from behind the house.

" Bite him, Prince! " exclaimed Herbert, triumphantly.

Prince needed no second invitation. Like the majority of dogs of respectable connections, he had a deep distrust and hatred of any person looking like a beggar or a tramp, and he sprang for the rough-looking visitor, barking furiously.

If Herbert expected the tramp to take flight it was because he did not know the courage and ferocity of Mike Hogan. Some dogs, doubtless, would have made him quail, but Prince was a small-sized dog, weighing not over fifty pounds, and, as the animal rushed to attack him, Mike gave a derisive laugh.

"Why don't you send a rat or a kitten?" he exclaimed, scornfully.

Prince was so accustomed to inspire fear that he did not stop to take the measure of his human adversary, but sprang over the fence and made for the tramp, intending to fasten his teeth in the leg of the latter.

But Mike Hogan was on the alert. He bent over, and, as the dog approached, dexterously seized him, threw him over on his back, and then commenced powerfully compressing his throat and choking him.

Poor Prince seemed utterly powerless in his vigorous grasp. His tongue protruded from his mouth, his eyes seemed starting from their sockets, and death by strangulation seemed imminent.

Herbert Ross surveyed this unexpected sight with mingled surprise and dismay.

"Let him go! Don't kill him!" he screamed.

"What made you set him on me?" demanded the tramp, savagely.

"Let him go, and he shan't bite you!" said Herbert.

"I will take care of that myself," said

Hogan. "When I get through with him, you'll have to bury him."

"Let him go, and I'll give you a quarter," said Herbert, in the extremity of his alarm.

"That sounds better," said Mike Hogan, moderating his grip. "Where's the quarter?"

Herbert hurried to the fence and handed over the coin.

Mike took it, and, with a laugh, tossed the almost senseless dog into the yard, where he lay gasping for breath.

"If you've got any more dogs, bring 'em on," he said, with a laugh. "Next time, you'll know how to treat a gentleman."

Herbert had a retort on the end of his tongue, but did not dare to utter it. He had been too much impressed and terrified by the tramp's extraordinary display of strength to venture to provoke him further.

"Well," thought Hogan, chuckling, "I made the boy come down with something, after all. I paid him well for his impudence."

Continuing on his way he stopped at a house where he was offered some cold meat, but no money. Being hungry, he accepted, and again continued his march.

In passing Mrs. Gordon's house his attention was attracted by the sound of voices. Thinking it possible that he might hear something which he could turn to advantage, he placed himself in a position where he could overhear what was said.

His eyes sparkled when he heard Miss Sally speak of the large sum of money she had in the house.

" Ho, ho! " said he, to himself, " I'm in luck. You won't need to carry that money to the bank, my lady. I'll take care of it for you. As for this boy who is to guard it, I'll scare him out of his wits! "

When Sally Peabody left the cottage of Mrs. Gordon she was not aware that her steps were tracked by one of the most reckless and desperate criminals in the State.

He followed her far enough to learn where she lived and then concealed himself in the woods until the time should come for active operations.

* * *

CHAPTER XIII.

ANDY ON GUARD.

THE Peabody girls, as people in Hamilton were accustomed to call them, though they were over fifty years of age, lived in an old-fashioned house, consisting of a main part and an L.

It was a prim-looking house, and everything about it looked prim; but nothing could be more neat and orderly. The front yard was in perfect order. Not a stick or a stone was out of place.

In the fall, when the leaves fell from the trees, they were carefully gathered every morning and carried away, for even nature was not allowed to make a litter on the old maids' premises.

A brass knocker projected from the outer door. The Misses Peabody had not yet adopted the modern innovation of bells. On either side of the front door was a square room—one serving as a parlor, the other as a sitting-room. In the rear of the latter was a kitchen, and in the rear of that was a woodshed. The last two rooms were in the L part. This L part consisted of a single story, surmounted by a gently-sloping roof. From the chamber over the sitting-room one could look out upon the roof of the L part.

This the reader will please to remember.

When Andy knocked at the door at five o'clock, it was opened by Miss Sally Peabody in person.

"I am so glad you have come, Andy," she said, "and so is sister Susan. I never said anything to her about inviting you, but she thought it a capital idea. We shall feel ever so much safer."

Of course Andy felt flattered by the importance assigned to his presence. What boy of his age would not?

"I don't know whether I can do any good, Miss Sally," he said, "but I am very glad to come."

"You shan't be sorry for it," assured Miss Susan, nodding significantly.

Probably this referred to her promise to pay Andy for his trouble. Our hero would never have asked anything for his service. Still, as the Peabodys were rich—that is, for a country village—he had no objection to receive anything which they might voluntarily offer.

"Come right in, Andy," said Miss Sally.

She preceded our hero into the sitting-room, where her sister Susan was setting the table for tea.

"Here he is, Susan—here is Andy," said Sally.

Andy received a cordial welcome from the elder of the two sisters.

"And how is your mother, Andy?" she asked.

"Pretty well, thank you, Miss Susan," answered Andy, surveying with interest the nice plate of hot biscuit which Miss Susan was placing on the tea table.

He was a healthy boy, and was growing

fast, so that he may be pardoned for appreciating a good table.

"We don't always have hot biscuits, Andy," said the simple-minded old maid, "but we thought you would like them, and so I told sister Sally that I would make some."

"I hope you haven't put yourself out any on my account, Miss Susan," Andy said.

"It isn't often we have company," said Susan, with a smile, "and we ought to have something a little better than common."

"I am not used to luxurious living, you know," said Andy.

"How is your mother getting along?" inquired his hostess, sympathetically.

"Very well, thank you!"

"My sister told me Mr. Starr was giving her some trouble."

"That is true; but I guess it'll turn out all right."

"If it doesn't," said Sally, "remember what I told your mother. My sister quite agrees with me that we will advance the money to pay the note, if necessary."

"You are very kind, Miss Sally, but you might never get it back."

"We will trust your mother—and you, Andy," said Sally Peabody, kindly. "It wouldn't ruin us if we did lose the money—would it, Sister Susan?"

" No, indeed ! " said Susan. " We shouldn't borrow any trouble on that account. But supper is ready. I hope you have an appetite, Andy? "

" I generally have," answered Andy, as he seated himself at the neat supper-table.

Our hero, whether he was in danger from burglars or not, was in danger of being made sick by the overflowing hospitality of the sisters. They so plied him with hot biscuits, cake, preserves and pie that our hero felt uncomfortable when he rose from the table. Even then his hospitable entertainers did not seem to think he had eaten enough.

" Why, you haven't made a supper, Andy," said Miss Sally.

" I don't think I ever ate so much in my life before at a single meal," answered Andy. " If you don't mind, I'll go out and walk a little."

" Certainly, Andy, if you wish."

Andy went out and walked about the place.

" How lucky the Peabodys are ! " he said to himself. " They have plenty to live upon, and don't have to earn a cent. I wonder how it would seem if mother and I were as well off? But they're very kind ladies, and I don't grudge them their good fortune, even if I am poor myself."

In one respect Andy was mistaken. It is

by no means a piece of good luck to be able to live without work. It takes away, in many cases, the healthy stimulus to action, and leaves life wearisome and monotonous.

More than one young man has been ruined by what the world called his good fortune.

In the corner of a small stable, Andy found a musket. Like most boys, he was attracted by a gun.

"I wonder whether it's loaded?" he said to himself.

He raised it to his shoulder and pulled the trigger.

Instantly there was a deafening report, and the two old maids ran to the door in dire dismay.

"What's the matter?" they cried, simultaneously, peeping through a crack of the door.

"I was trying this gun," said Andy, a little ashamed.

"A gun! Where did it come from?"

"Isn't it yours?"

"No; we wouldn't dare to keep a gun about. Why, where did you find it?"

Andy told them, and they concluded it had been left by a neighbor, who had recently done a little work around the place.

Andy was struck by an idea.

"May I take it into the house," he asked,

"and keep it in the chamber where I am to sleep?"

"I shouldn't dare to have a gun in the house," said Susan.

"But it isn't loaded."

"I think there is no objection," said Sally, who was not quite so timid as her sister. "We are going to put you into the chamber over the sitting-room," she added.

"All right!" said Andy.

"The money is in a little trunk under your bed. You won't be afraid to have it there, will you?"

"I am never afraid of money," said Andy, smiling.

Andy went to bed at an early hour—at about quarter after nine. It was the custom of the sisters to go to bed early, and he did not wish to interfere with their household arrangements.

The gun he placed in the corner of the room, close to his bed.

He did not know how long he had been asleep, when, all at once, he awoke suddenly. The moonlight was streaming into the room, and by the help of it he saw a villainous-looking face jammed against the pane of the window overlooking the shed.

"A burglar!" thought he, and sprang from the bed.

CHAPTER XIV.

ANDY IS BESIEGED.

My readers will admit that to awaken from sleep, and see a man looking in at the window, is sufficient to startle a brave man. When it is added that the face bore the unmistakable mark of bad passions and a lawless life, it will be understood that Andy might well have been excused for momentary terror.

He was, however, partly prepared for the visit by the knowledge that there was money in the house, which he was especially commissioned to guard. Still, he had not really supposed there was any danger of a burglar coming to so quiet a village as Hamilton in pursuit of money.

Besides, no one but himself, so he supposed, knew that the maiden ladies had a large sum of money in their dwelling.

I will not deny that Andy was startled— I will not admit that he was frightened, for this is inconsistent with his conduct.

He certainly had not awakened any too soon. There was not a minute to lose. The burglar was trying to raise the window, preparatory to entering the room.

In this, however, he met with a difficulty.

The window was fastened at the middle, and he could not raise it.

"Curse the bolt!" exclaimed the disappointed burglar. "I shall have to smash it in!"

Just then, however, Andy sprang from the bed, and, under the circumstances, Hogan felt glad. He could frighten the boy into turning the fastening, and admitting him.

As Andy rose, he grasped the old musket, and, not without a thrill of excitement, faced the scoundrel.

If the gun had been loaded, he would have felt safe, but he knew very well that he could do no harm with it.

Mike Hogan saw the gun, but he was not a coward, and he felt convinced that Andy would not dare to use it, though he supposed it to be loaded.

"What do you want?" called out Andy, in a firm voice.

"Open this window!" cried Hogan, in a tone of command.

He was not afraid of being heard by other parties, on account of the isolated position of the house.

As he spoke, he tugged at the frame of the window; but, of course, without success.

"Why should I?" returned Andy, who wanted time to think.

"Never mind, you young jackanapes. Do as I tell you!" said Hogan, fiercely.

As he spoke, overcome by his irritation at being foiled when close upon the treasure he coveted, he smashed a pane with his fist, but not without cutting his hand and drawing blood.

Through the fractured pane Andy could hear him more distinctly.

"What do you want?" repeated Andy.

"I want that five hundred dollars you are guarding, and I mean to have it!" returned Hogan.

"What five hundred dollars?" asked Andy, but he could not help being startled by the accurate information of the burglar.

"Oh, you needn't play ignorant!" said Hogan, impatiently. "The lady who lives here sent for you to take care of it. She might as well have engaged a baby," he added, contemptuously.

"You will find I am something more than a baby!" said Andy, stoutly.

"Open this window, I tell you once again."

"I won't!" said Andy, shortly.

"You won't, hey? Do you know what I will do with you when I get in?" demanded Hogan, furiously.

"No, I don't."

" I'll beat you black and blue."

" You'll have to get in first," said our hero, undaunted.

" Do you think I can't? "

Hogan spoke with assumed confidence, but he realized that it would not be easy if Andy held out. He had already had a severe experience in breaking one pane of glass, and shrank from trying another.

" I know you can't," said Andy, and he raised the gun significantly to his shoulder and held it pointed toward the burglar.

" Put down that gun! " shouted Hogan.

" Then leave the window."

" Just wait till I get at you," said Hogan, grinding his teeth.

He realized that Andy was not as easily scared as he anticipated. To be balked by a mere boy was galling to him. If he only had a pistol himself; but he had none. He had had one when he left New York, but he had sold it for two dollars, fifty miles away. He was positively helpless, while Andy had him at a disadvantage. Should he give up his intended robbery? That would be a bitter disappointment, for he was penniless, and five hundred dollars would be a great windfall for him. An idea came to him.

" Put down your gun," he said, in a milder

tone. " I have something to propose to you."

In some surprise, Andy complied with his request.

" There are five hundred dollars in this house."

" You say so," said Andy, non-committally.

" Pooh! I know there are. That is a large sum of money."

" I suppose it is," said Andy, who did not understand his drift.

So is half of it. Two hundred and fifty dollars would be a big sum for a boy like you."

" What have I to do with it? " asked Andy, puzzled.

" Open this window and let me in, and I'll share the money with you."

" Oh, that's what you mean, is it? "

" Yes. No one need know that you have part of the money. It will be thought that I have made off with all of it."

" Then you think I am a thief, like yourself? " exclaimed Andy, indignantly. " You are very much mistaken. Even if this money were in the house, I wouldn't take a cent of it."

" Oh, you're mighty honest! And I'm a thief, am I? " sneered Hogan, surveying our hero with an ugly look.

" Yes," answered Andy.

"You'll repent your impudence," said Hogan, with a vindictive scowl.

As he spoke, he enlarged the hole in the pane, and, putting in his hand, attempted, by thrusting it upward, to unlock the fastening.

Had he succeeded in doing this, he could have raised the window easily, and, once in the chamber, our young hero would have been no match for him.

Andy realized this, and saw that he must act instantly.

He brought down the butt end of the musket on the intruding hand with all his strength, the result being a howl of pain from the burglar.

"You'd better give that up," said Andy, his eyes flashing with excitement.

Somehow all his timidity had vanished, and he was firmly resolved to defend the property intrusted to his charge as long as his strength or shrewdness enabled him to do so.

"Your life shall pay for this," exclaimed the injured burglar, with a terrible oath.

Andy realized that he would fare badly if he should fall into the clutches of the villain, whose face was actually distorted by rage and pain. The extremity of his danger, however, only nerved him for continued resistance.

"Once more, will you open the window?" demanded Hogan, who would not have parleyed so long if he had known any way to get in without Andy's help.

"No, I won't!" answered Andy with resolution.

Mike Hogan surveyed the window, and considered whether it would be feasible to throw his burly frame against it, and so crush it in. Undoubtedly he could have done it had he been on the same level, but it was about three feet higher than he, and so the feat would be more difficult. Besides, it would be a work of time, and Andy, in whom he found much more boldness than he anticipated, might shoot him.

A thought came to him, and he began to descend the sloping roof.

"What is he going to do now?" thought Andy. "Has he given it up as a bad job?"

This was a point which he could not determine.

CHAPTER XV.

AN EXCITING SCENE.

HOGAN had not given it up as a bad job. Andy's unexpected resistance only made him the more determined to effect his object. Besides the natural desire to obtain so large a booty, he thirsted for revenge upon Andy.

"The boy's plucky!" he muttered, as he descended from the roof; "but I'll be even with him yet."

He had to descend cautiously, for the shingles were slippery, but he finally reached the lowest point and jumped down.

"If I could only find an ax or a hatchet," he said to himself, "I would make short work of the window. I don't believe the boy will dare to shoot."

He searched for the articles he had named, but in vain.

"What can I take?" he thought, perplexed.

His eyes fell upon a thick club, not unlike a baseball bat, and this seemed to him suitable for his purpose. He took it and commenced reascending to the roof again. There was a fence, which helped him as a stepping-stone, otherwise he would have found it difficult to get a footing upon it. Meanwhile Andy had not been idle.

First of all, he saw that it was unsafe to have the money any longer in his custody. His assailant might be successful in the new attempt he would probably make, and he must not find the bank bills.

Andy did not like to frighten the ladies, but he thought it necessary, under the circumstances. He went to the door of the parlor chamber, which the two sisters occupied, and rapped loudly on the door.

The knock was heard, and it excited dismay. The timid ladies thought it might be the burglar of whom they were so much in fear.

" Who's there? " asked Miss Susan, in trembling accents, through the keyhole.

" It's me—Andy. Please open the door— quick ! "

" What has happened? " demanded Miss Susan, in agitation.

" I want to hand you the trunk," answered Andy.

" What for? Is there any burglar in the house? "

" No; but there's one trying to get into my room."

" Oh, heavens! what shall we do? " ejaculated both ladies, in chorus.

" Take the tin trunk, and I'll manage him," said Andy.

The door was opened a crack and the trunk taken into the trembling hands of the agitated spinster.

" Where is the burglar? " answered Susan.

" Gone to find something to break through the window."

" Oh, dear, he will murder us all ! "

" No, he won't," said Andy. " I won't let him ! "

"You'd better hide," said Susan. "Is he a big man?"

"Pretty large. He looks as if he was just out of jail."

"He mustn't hurt you. I'd rather he had the money. Take it and give it to him and ask him to go."

"Not much!" answered Andy, stoutly. "But I must go. He'll soon be at the window again. Is there any hot water in the house?"

"Yes; we keep a fire all night in the kitchen, and the teakettle is full."

"All right!" said Andy, and he dashed downstairs.

"What's he going to do?" ejaculated Susan, in surprise.

"Heaven only knows! How can he talk of hot water when there's a burglar in the house? Lock the door, Sister Susan."

"I don't like to shut out poor Andy," said Susan, in a distressed voice. It's my belief we shall find him a mangled corpse to-morrow morning, when we go downstairs."

"I shan't dare to go down at all. Oh, Susan, this is awful!"

Leaving the agitated spinsters in their trouble and terror, we must look after Andy. He ran downstairs, seized the teakettle from the stove, grabbed a tin dipper, and then ran up to his chamber again.

He was just in time.

There, before the window, stood Mike Hogan, with the club in his hand and a look of triumph on his face. In the dim light, he did not see the teakettle.

"Well, my little bantam," said he, "here I am again!"

"So I see," said Andy, coolly.

"Once more, and for the last time, I ask you to open that window."

"I would rather not."

"You will, if you know what is best for yourself. Do you see this club?"

"Yes, I do."

"Do you know what it is for?"

"Suppose you tell me."

"It is to break open the window."

"That is what I thought."

"Comfound the boy! He's a cool customer," thought Hogan. "Bah! he must be a fool. Open that window, and I'll give you ten dollars of the money," he said, preferring, if possible, to avoid all trouble.

Of course, when he was fairly in possession of the money, he could break his promise and give Andy a beating, and he proposed to do both.

"A little while ago you offered me half the money," said Andy.

"Things were different then. I didn't have this club. What do you say?"

"That I am not a thief, and don't mean to make a bargain with a thief!" answered Andy, resolutely.

"Then you may take the consequences, you young rascal!" exploded the burglar, garnishing his speech with an oath.

"In two minutes, I shall have you in my clutches!"

He swung back the club and brought it down with full force upon the window frame. Of course, the panes were shivered and the frail wooden sticks which constituted the frame were demolished. Another blow and the window lay in ruins on the carpet of Andy's chamber.

"He's killing Andy!" ejaculated the terrified spinsters, as the loud noise came to their ears. "What shall we do?"

They debated whether they should leave their chamber, and, seeking the scene of the tragedy, fall down on their knees before the terrible burglar and implore him to spare the life of their young defender. The spirit was willing, but the flesh was weak, and in terrible agitation they remained in their sanctuary.

"The crisis has come," thought Andy, his nerves quivering with excitement.

And, unobserved by the triumphant burglar, he poured out the scalding hot water from the teakettle into the tin dipper.

Mike Hogan was in the act of scaling the window-sill, over the debris of the broken glass and wood, when Andy dashed the contents of the tin dipper into his face.

There was a fearful yell as the hot water deluged his face and neck, and the scalded burglar, losing his hold on the sill, blinded and maddened by pain, lost his footing and slipped down the sloping roof with ever-increasing rapidity. He rolled over at the eaves, and fell upon his back with a violence which lamed, though it did not disable him—a thoroughly demoralized burglar.

There was a pump and a trough in the yard. Hogan jumped up and ran hastily to it. He dipped his scalded face in the stream of water, and gained temporary relief. But the pain was altogether too great to allow him to think of anything else except that. To a man in his condition, money had no charms. A relief from pain was all he could think of. Again and again he dipped his face in the cool water, and his pain was somewhat abated.

"Oh, the young villain!" he groaned. "I

wish I had him here. I'd tear him limb from limb."

"Poor fellow!" thought Andy, pitying the poor wretch, though the imminent danger had forced him to inflict suffering upon him. "I am sorry for his pain, but I couldn't defend myself in any other way. He won't try to get in again, I'm thinking."

He locked the door of the room from the outside, and decided to spend the rest of the night upon the sofa in the sitting-room. First, however, he went to the room of the old ladies, to tell them that the danger was past.

CHAPTER XVI.

EXCITEMENT IN THE VILLAGE.

FOR the remainder of the night, Andy, as the saying is, slept with one eye open. The burglar had enough to think of, and it seemed very unlikely that he would make another attempt to enter the house. Still, Andy thought it best to watch him.

Through the window he could see Hogan dipping his face again and again in the trough. This continued for perhaps half an hour. Then he slowly left the yard, but not without shaking his fist at the house which contained the young hero who had balked him in his unlawful designs. To be brief, for the remainder of the night the house had rest.

Early in the morning the two sisters came downstairs. Andy, who had dressed himself, to be prepared for an emergency, was lying on the sofa, sleeping peacefully.

" Poor boy! " murmured Susan. " What a terrible night he must have passed! "

" And all in our defense, too. I never dreamed that he was so brave."

" It's a mercy the burglar didn't carry him off."

" It was the money he wanted, sister."

" But he might have killed Andy."

" That is true. It seems to me, sister, we ought to pay him handsomely for what he has done."

" I am quite of your opinion, Sister Sally. How much do you think we ought to give him? "

" I wouldn't do what he did for fifty dollars."

" Shall it be fifty dollars, then? "

" If you are willing."

" I am quite willing. Do you dare to go up with me into the chamber overhead? "

" I don't know. It makes me tremble to think of it."

Finally the two sisters mustered the necessary courage and cautiously crept upstairs, and paused before the door, which was locked upon the outside.

"Suppose the wicked man is inside?" suggested Susan, trembling.

"Oh, there is no fear! He wouldn't care to stay after he found the money gone."

With some apprehension, they opened the door. When they saw the wreck of glass and wood upon the carpet, they raised their hands in dismay.

"What a terrible fight poor Andy must have had!" said Susan.

"He has done better than a man," exclaimed Sally, enthusiastically.

I am inclined to think that Miss Sally was right, and that many men would have displayed less boldness and shrewdness than our young hero.

"Why, here is the teakettle!" said Sally. "How in the world did it come here?"

"And here is the tin dipper. Well, Andy will tell us when he wakes up. We must give him a good breakfast. He deserves it, after all he has done."

At eight o'clock, Andy sat down to a nice breakfast. It seemed that neither of the two ladies could express sufficient gratitude, or induce him to eat enough.

"But for you, Andy, we might have been murdered in our beds."

"I don't think so," answered Andy, modestly; "but I think you would have lost your money."

"That we should! Now tell us all about it."

So Andy told the story, amid exclamations of wonder and admiration from the two sisters.

"How in the world could the man know we had so much money in the house?" said Susan, in wonder.

"He seemed to know just how much there was," said Andy. "He mentioned the amount. I think he must have overheard one of you speaking of it."

"I didn't really suppose there was any burglar about," said Sally. "How lucky it was that we engaged you to come and stay here!"

Andy was modest, but he could not, with truth, disclaim this praise. He knew very well that he had been instrumental, under Providence, in saving the old ladies from being robbed.

"I don't know whether you would be willing to stay here to-night, Andy, after the experience you had last night," said Sally.

"Oh, yes!"

" And you are not afraid? "

" I don't think the man will come again," said Andy, laughing. " I don't believe he liked the reception I gave him. He knows how it feels to get into hot water."

It is needless to say that the news of the midnight attack upon the house of the Peabody sisters spread like wildfire through the village.

Probably not less than a hundred persons called to see the demolished window, and Andy had to tell the story over and over till he was weary of it.

Among those who were interested was Herbert Ross. He suspected, and rightly, that it was the same man who had stopped at his father's gate, and nearly strangled his dog Prince.

He felt that if this was so, a part of the public interest would center upon him, and accordingly, forgetting his recent difficulty with Andy, he cross-questioned our hero as to the appearance of the burglar.

" Did he have black hair? " he asked.

" Yes."

" And a face that had not been shaved for a week? "

" Yes; as well as I could see in the dim light."

" And wasn't very tall? "

" No; he was rather short and thickset, with a ragged suit of clothes."

" It's the very man that called at our house ! " exclaimed Herbert, in excitement.

Of course, he was questioned, and gave an account of the call of Hogan, in which he appeared to considerably greater advantage than he had actually done.

" He was very impudent," said Herbert, boastfully; " but I gave him to understand that I would have him arrested if he didn't 'leave pretty quick."

" Did that frighten him? " asked a neighbor, with a queer smile.

" Oh, yes," said Herbert. " He saw that he had hold of the wrong customer, and tramped off in a different direction."

" What would you have done if you had been in Andy's place last night? "

" I wouldn't have let him in."

" But do you think you could have driven him off? "

" Certainly," answered Herbert, confidently. " Andy did very well," he added, condescendingly; " but I should have succeeded as well in keeping the rascal out of the house."

" Why don't you offer to stay at the house to-night? No doubt, Andy will be glad to rest? "

"I don't let myself out for any such purpose," said Herbert, hastily. "He is a poor boy, and needs the money. You wouldn't expect a gentleman's son to engage in any such business?"

"Andy is a gentleman's son. If ever there was a gentleman, Mr. Gordon was one."

"No doubt he was a very worthy man," said Herbert, patronizingly; "but that isn't what I mean."

Herbert succeeded in his wish to draw attention to himself, and told the story of his encounter with the tramp and burglar many times—adding a little every time—till, by dint of repetitions, he persuaded himself that he had acted a very heroic part, and was entitled to share the honors of the day with Andy.

Unlike our hero, he was perfectly willing to tell the story over and over as many times as he could obtain a fresh auditor.

On Monday morning, Andy's guard was over; but there was still a service which the old ladies desired of him.

The money was to be deposited in the Cranston Bank, located six miles away. There was no railroad connecting the two places, and the road was a lonely one, extending part of the way through the woods.

On previous occasions, the ladies had themselves gone to the bank, when they had occasion to deposit money, but the recent attempt at burglary had so terrified them that they felt afraid to venture.

In their emergency, they thought of Andy, and asked him if he would be willing to drive over and carry the money with him.

" Oh, yes! " answered Andy, who was fond of driving. " I couldn't go till I had attended to my duties at the academy, but I should be through by nine o'clock."

" That would be early enough. But you would lose school."

" Only for half a day, and Dr. Euclid would excuse me."

So it was arranged that Andy was to carry the five hundred dollars to the Cranston Bank.

CHAPTER XVII.

PREPARING FOR A JOURNEY.

CRANSTON was six miles away—too far to walk. The Misses Peabody did not keep a horse. Indeed, one would have been of very little use to them, for both were timid, and neither would have been willing to drive.

" You are not afraid to drive to Cranston, Andy? " said Miss Sally.

"No; what should I be afraid of?" asked our hero.

"You are not timid about horses, then?"

Andy laughed.

"I should think not," he replied. "I only wish mother could afford to keep a horse."

I think they are terrible creatures. They are so strong, and sometimes they are so contrary," said Miss Susan, with a shudder.

"Then you should use the whip on them, Miss Susan."

"I wouldn't dare to."

"Well, I'm not afraid. I only wish I were in Add Bean's place. He is driving around every day with his father's horse."

The boy referred to—Addison Bean, called Add, for short—was one of Andy's schoolmates at the academy, and was quite as fond of driving as Andy himself.

"I wonder if we couldn't engage Mr. Bean's horse and carriage? Will you see?"

"Yes; it is a good one, and I should like to drive it."

Andy called at Mr. Bean's and succeeded in his errand. The horse was to be ready for him at nine o'clock.

"What are you going to Cranston for, Andy?" asked Mr. Bean.

"To the bank, for the Peabody girls."

That's what all the villagers call them, in spite of their age.

"Then I suppose you will carry money with you?"

"Yes."

"Don't let anybody know your errand, then."

"Do you think there is any danger?"

"There is always danger when a man is supposed to be carrying money. A boy is still more in danger."

"I won't tell anybody my errand."

"You haven't seen anything of that burglar you scalded the other night?"

"No."

"I should like to have been near at the time."

"I wish you had," said Andy.

Mr. Bean was a deputy sheriff, and a strong, powerful man, who had more than once been called upon to arrest noted criminals.

Mr. Bean gave Andy another suggestion, which proved of value to him. What it was, the reader will ascertain in due time.

Andy got into the carriage—a buggy—and drove round to the house of the maiden ladies. He fastened the horse at the fence, and, opening the gate, went in.

"Have you got the money ready, Miss Peabody?" he asked, addressing Miss Susan.

"Here it is, Andy—four hundred and fifty dollars."

"But I thought," said Andy, in surprise, "that there were five hundred dollars?"

The two sisters looked at each other significantly.

"We have another use for fifty dollars," said Miss Sally.

"All right!" said Andy, who did not suppose that this was a matter with which he had anything to do.

"In fact," she continued, "we are going to give it to you."

"Going to give me fifty dollars?" Andy exclaimed, in amazement.

"Yes."

And here Miss Susan spoke.

"We feel that it is due to you on account of the bravery you showed the other night."

"I thank you very much!" said Andy, quite overwhelmed at this munificence; "but it is altogether too much for me to receive."

"We are the judges of that. You can make good use of the money, or your mother can, and we shan't miss it."

Andy knew that both these statements were quite true, and he thankfully accepted the generous gift. It was arranged that he should call and get it on his return from the bank.

CHAPTER XVIII.

THE RIDE TO CRANSTON.

ANDY set out on his trip in high spirits. It was a fine morning. The air was pleasant and bracing, and the sun shed a flood of glory over the landscape.

Andy enjoyed school and school studies, but nevertheless it did seem to him that there was more pleasure in riding over the hills to Cranston than in poring over the pages of Virgil in Dr. Euclid's classroom.

Then again, it was a rare pleasure for him to have the guidance of a horse. His mother had never been able to keep one, and though now and then he got a chance to ride with a neighbor, it occurred but seldom. Sometimes his friend and schoolmate, Add Bean, took him in, but was generally reluctant to yield the reins, being fond of driving himself.

There was another cause for his high spirits. The handsome present which he had just received he looked upon as a veritable windfall. Fifty dollars in his mother's economical establishment would go a good way. It would enable them to buy some necessary articles which otherwise must be dispensed with. For instance, Andy himself needed a new suit very much, but he had not troubled his mother with asking for one, because he didn't know where the money was to come from to buy it.

When the money contained in his father's wallet arrived, he was somewhat encouraged, but now with this fresh supply there was no doubt that he would feel justified in spending a part for the needed suit.

" I wonder what has become of the burglar?" thought Andy, as he rode smoothly along the road. " Wouldn't he like to know where I am going, and on what errand? He would find it easier to master me here than he did the other night."

Scarcely had this thought passed through his mind when he was hailed by a stranger whom he had just passed on the road.

It was a young man, slender and well dressed, with a ready smile and a set of dazzling white teeth. He would be considered good looking, but his face was not one to inspire confidence in a thoughtful observer.

" My young friend, are you going to Cranston?"

" Yes," answered Andy.

" So am I. Is it far?"

" About five miles from here."

Andy had already gone a mile on his way.

" Five miles! Whew! that is a distance. I say, haven't you got room for one more? "

Ordinarily Andy would have been entirely willing to take in a passenger, being naturally sociable and obliging, but now he was made cautious by the nature of his errand and the knowledge of the large sum of money which he was carrying. He halted his horse and looked perplexed.

" Come, be obliging," said the stranger, with affected frankness.

" You are a stranger," said Andy, hesitatingly.

" Well, suppose I am. I haven't got the smallpox or any other contagious disorder," laughed the young man.

" I wasn't thinking of that."

" Come, you don't mind making a little money. I'll give you a dollar if you'll give me a ride."

" It isn't worth a dollar," said Andy, honestly.

" Oh, I don't insist upon paying so much! If you'll take me for fifty cents, all the better."

" I might as well," thought Andy. " Of course, he can know nothing of my errand, and it's an easy way to earn fifty cents. I don't want to be too cowardly. " Well," he said, after a pause, " I'll take you. Jump in! "

" Enough said," returned the other.

And he lost no time in availing himself of the invitation.

They talked together on indifferent topics till Andy reached the lonely part of the road already referred to, when a sudden change came over his companion.

" Now to business!" he said, in a quick, stern voice. " Give me that money you have in your pocket, and be quick about it!"

Turning hastily, Andy confronted a pistol in the hands of his companion. It was held within six inches of his head, and might well have startled an older person than Andy.

CHAPTER XIX.

FOILING A HIGHWAYMAN.

OF course Andy was startled when he saw the pistol in close proximity to his head. I feel no hesitation in admitting that he felt far from comfortable. Some heroes are represented as startled by nothing, and afraid of nothing; but though Andy was unusually self-possessed for his years, he was not above the ordinary emotions of humanity.

Still, he did not lose his presence of mind utterly, nor was he willing to surrender at discretion, though it did occur to him that he was in an uncommonly tight place.

More for the sake of gaining time to think than because he really needed the information, he asked, with a calmness which he did not feel:

"What do you mean, sir?"

"What do I mean?" repeated his companion, with a sneer. "If you are not a fool, you ought to know what I mean."

"I suppose you are playing a joke on me," said Andy, innocently.

"Does this look like a joke?" asked the young man, with a significant nod at the pistol which he held in his hand.

"Is it loaded?" asked Andy.

"Loaded?" retorted the other. "I could blow off the roof of your head with it."

"I hope you won't, then," said our hero, looking anxiously in advance, hoping to see some approaching vehicle.

If so, he would be safe, for his companion, desperate though he might be, would not venture in that case to risk capture and the long term of imprisonment to which such a daring attempt at highway robbery would expose him to.

"I have no time for fooling!" said the young man, sharply. "Give me that money you have in your possession, or it will be the worse for you."

"What money?" asked Andy.

"The money you are carrying to Cranston to deposit in the bank for the old women in Hamilton."

"Where could he have found out about it?" thought Andy. "I wish somebody would come along."

Anything to gain time!

"Pray don't take it from me, Mr. Robber!" said Andy, pretending to be overcome with terror. "They will think I took it."

"I can't help that."

"And they will have me put in jail. Oh, don't take it from me!"

"The boy is pretty well scared," said the robber to himself. "I didn't think he would wilt down so easily. He seems a little soft."

"I'll attend to that," he said aloud. "I'll write them an anonymous letter, saying that I took it from you."

"That will be better," said Andy, seeming relieved.

"Then hand it over."

"I won't exactly give it to you," said Andy; "but you can take it."

So saying, he drew a large wallet from his inside pocket, and, before his companion could grasp it, threw it some rods away by the road-side.

"There," he said; "you see I didn't give it to you, though I can't help your taking it."

His companion's eyes glistened as he saw the plethoric wallet lying by the roadside.

"Stop the horse!" he exclaimed, jerking at the reins. "I'll get out here."

"All right!" said Andy. "You'll be sure to write to Miss Peabody that I couldn't help giving you the money?"

"Oh, yes! What a simpleton he is!" thought the highwayman, as he sprang from the buggy, and hurried in the direction of the wallet, now some little distance back.

As soon as he had gotten rid of his companion, Andy brought down his whip with emphasis on the back of his spirited horse, and dashed over the road at great speed.

The young man smiled as he heard the flying wheels.

"He's pretty well scared," he thought. "Well, he can go to Cranston as fast as he pleases, now that I have what I was after."

He stooped and picked up the wallet, and opened it to feast his eyes on the thick roll of bank bills, but was overcome with rage, fury and disappointment when he found that the supposed treasure consisted only of rolls of brown paper, so folded as to swell out the wallet and give the impression of value.

"The artful young scoundrel!" he exclaimed, between his closed teeth. "He has made a fool of me, and I all the time looked upon him as a simpleton. What shall I say to Hogan, who put me up to this job?"

He had a momentary idea of pursuing Andy, but by this time the buggy was a long distance ahead, and every minute was increasing the distance.

To pursue it with any expectation of overtaking it would have been the merest folly. It was hard to give up so rich a prize, but there seemed no help for it.

"I wish I could wring the young rascal's neck," thought the baffled highwayman. "He was fooling me all the time, and now he is chuckling over the trick he has played upon me. How shall I meet Hogan?"

The young man hesitated a moment, and then plunged into the woods that skirted the road.

Continuing his walk for five minutes, he came to a secluded spot, where, under a tree, reclined an old acquaintance of ours—in brief, Mr. Michael Hogan.

Hogan's face was red and inflamed, and his eyes were sore. He was suffering from the severe scalding which had rewarded his attempt to enter the house of the Misses Peabody.

He looked up quickly as he heard the approach of his confederate, and demanded, eagerly:

"Well, Bill, did you see the boy?"

"Yes, I saw him."

"And you have got the money?" asked Hogan, with like eagerness.

"I have got that," answered the younger man, as he displayed the deceptive wallet.

"Give it to me."

"You are welcome to all you can find in it."

Hogan opened the wallet quickly. When he saw the contents, he turned upon his confederate with lowering brow.

"What does this mean?" he demanded, in a harsh voice.

"It means that I have been fooled," said Bill, bitterly.

"Who has fooled you?" asked Hogan, with an angry look.

"The boy! I tell you, Hogan, he's a smart one."

"I don't understand this. I believe you are deceiving me," said the older man, suspiciously.

"Think what you please," said Bill, sullenly. "It is as I say."

"Didn't you take out the bills and replace them with worthless paper?"

"No, I didn't.   I wouldn't dare play such a trick on you.   I know you are a desperate and reckless man, and I wouldn't try it."

"Then will you explain this foolery?" said Hogan, sharply.   "Why did you let the boy palm off this worthless paper on you?"

"I'll tell you all about it," said Bill, convinced that his personal safety required him to allay the evident suspicion of the old man.

Thereupon he told the story, which is already familiar to the reader.

"You're a fool!" said Hogan, with bitter harshness.   "Bah! are you not a match for a boy of sixteen?"

"He may be only sixteen," said Bill, doggedly; "but he's no baby, I can tell you that! As to not being a match for him, you know something about that."

Mike Hogan sprang to his feet, livid with fury at this allusion to what was, with him, a very sore subject.

"If you dare to mention that affair again," he said, "I'll brain you!" and he looked quite capable of carrying out his threat.

"We ought to be revenged upon him," declared Bill, hurriedly, anxious to divert the wrath of the elder man into a channel less menacing to himself. " I have a plan——"

" Out with it! "

" The boy will have to come back along the same road."

" Well? "

" Let's lie in wait for him."

" But he will have deposited the money in the bank. It will do no good——"

" Not in the way of money, but you can be revenged upon him for the way he treated you the other night."

This allusion evoked another oath from the desperate and angry ruffian, but on the whole the plan pleased him. He thirsted for revenge upon the boy to whom he was indebted, not alone for foiling him in his attempted robbery, but who had entailed upon him so much physical suffering.

" There's something in that," he said. " If I get hold of him, I will give him something to remember me by! "

The lawless pair posted themselves near the road, yet in concealment, and waited impatiently for the return of Andy from the Cranston Bank.

CHAPTER XX.

PERKINS, THE DETECTIVE.

AFTER parting with his troublesome traveling companion, Andy lost no time in continuing on his way to the Cranston Bank, where he had the satisfaction of depositing the four hundred and fifty dollars which had been intrusted to him.

"I am glad to get rid of the money," said Andy, breathing a deep sigh of relief as he received back the bank-book.

"People are not usually glad to get rid of money," said the receiving teller.

"There is too much responsibility about it," said Andy. "Twice I have had a narrow escape from robbery."

"Were you the boy that proved more than a match for a burglar, Saturday night?" asked the teller, with interest.

"Have you heard of it, then?" asked Andy, in surprise.

"Oh, yes! Such news travels fast. We have every reason for informing ourselves of the movements of lawbreakers and burglars. You are a plucky boy."

"Thank you!" said Andy, modestly. "I don't know about that."

"Not many boys would have stood a midnight siege as well as you did."

"I was in more danger this morning," said Andy, quietly.

"How?" asked the teller and the other employees of the bank, who had heard Andy's statement, and came up to hear what he had to say.

"I was stopped by a highwayman this morning, on my way from Hamilton."

"You don't say so! Was it the same one?"

"No; it was a younger man. I suppose you haven't heard of that?" he added, smiling.

"No; we shall get our information from the chief actor in the adventure. How was it?"

Andy told his story, and the narration increased the high opinion which the bank officials already had begun to entertain of his courage and shrewdness.

"That was a capital idea—having a decoy wallet with you," said Mr. Smith, the receiving teller.

"It was not my idea, though," said Andy, modestly. "It was Mr. Bean who recommended it."

"The fellow must have been disappointed when he saw what he had captured," suggested the paying teller.

"I suppose he was," responded Andy, with a laugh, " but I didn't wait to find out. I gave the horse the whip, and left the place as fast as he could carry me."

"Are you not afraid the man may lie in wait for you on your way home?"

"I thought of that, but I have left the money here. It wouldn't do him any good to take the bank-book."

"That is true, but he may wish to be revenged upon you."

"That is so, but there is no help for it. There is no other road to take, and I must chance it."

Andy took the matter lightly, but it occurred to the bank officials that he stood in danger of being seriously injured.

"You ought not to go back alone," said the paying teller.

"Where shall I find company."

Just then a man entered the bank, and presented a check.

"The very man!" said the receiving teller. "He will go with you."

Andy looked at the newcomer, and was led to doubt whether such a man would be of much service to him. He was a short, slender man, of thirty-five, very quiet in his manner, with hair inclined to be red.

Andy knew many of the citizens of Cranston, but never remembered meeting with this man.

"Mr. Perkins," said the paying teller, "you heard of the attempted burglary at Hamilton on Saturday night?"

"Yes; that is partly what I came to this neighborhood about," answered Mr. Perkins, quietly.

"You see that boy?"

"Yes."

"It is the boy who defended the house and foiled the burglar."

Mr. Perkins dropped his air of quiet. His eyes and features betrayed a strong feeling of interest as he turned to Andy.

"My young friend," he said, "you are the very person I most wished to see. Will you answer me a few questions?"

"Yes, sir, with pleasure."

"What was the appearance of the man who attempted to enter the house where the money was kept?"

Andy gave, as nearly as he could, a description of Hogan and his peculiarities.

Perkins listened attentively, nodding from time to time with a satisfied expression.

"I know the man," he said. "I didn't think he was in this part of the country, but I am glad to hear that he is so near. I think I can put a spoke in his wheel."

"Who is it?" asked the paying teller.

"A man with more than one name. He is best known as Mike Hogan, though I am not sure whether this is his real name or not."

"I wonder if the other man is one of his friends?" said Andy, musingly.

"The other man?" repeated Mr. Perkins, inquiringly.

"Yes, the man that tried to rob me this morning."

"This is something new to me," returned the detective. "Was an attempt made upon you this morning?"

"Yes, sir."

"Tell me about it."

Of course, Andy gave for the second time an account of his morning's adventure.

The detective listened with the closest attention.

"Unquestionably the two men are in league together," he said.

"Have you any idea who the younger man is?" asked the teller.

"No; it may be any one of half a dozen. The description will fit quite a number of my acquaintances. My theory is that Hogan was near at hand when the attack was made, and that he instigated it. I presume that it was from him that the younger man learned that you were likely to come this way with the money in your possession."

" I didn't think of that," said Andy.

" Of course not. You know nothing of the ways of these gentry. The less you are compelled to know of them, the better for you. When are you going back?"

" I am ready now."

" We thought the boy might be stopped again," said Mr. Smith.

" It is altogether likely," said Mr. Perkins, quietly.

" And we recommended him not to go alone, as of course he would be no match for a man."

" He has proved himself a match in two instances," said Perkins, with a glance of approval at our hero. " Still, he might not always be so lucky. However, he won't be abliged to go back alone, as I will ask a seat in his carriage."

" I shall be very glad to have you come, sir," said Andy, politely.

" Can you wait fifteen minutes?"

" Oh, yes, sir!"

" I am staying at the hotel. I need to go there for a short time."

" All right, sir."

" Stay here, and I will join you very shortly."

The hotel was just across the street. Andy whiled away the time in the house, but he did not have to wait long.

A lady, neatly attired in an alpaca dress, entered from the street, and coming up to our hero, said:

" Are you ready? "

Andy stared at her in surprise.

She raised a green veil, and with some difficulty he recognized the features of Perkins, the detective.

" They won't be afraid of a woman," said Perkins, with a meaning smile. " Come along! "

CHAPTER XXI.

MIKE HOGAN'S CAPTURE.

THE sudden transformation of Perkins into a woman struck Andy with amazement. He knew nothing about detectives and their ways, and could not understand how the change had been effected so rapidly. Perkins enjoyed the boy's astonishment.

" I see you are surprised at my appearance," he remarked, with a smile.

" Yes, ma'am—I mean, sir."

"I assure you that I am a man," continued the detective, noticing his confusion.

"I was wondering where you got a dress to fit you so well," Andy ventured to say.

"Oh, I brought it with me!" said Perkins, composedly.

"Do you often dress up as a woman?"

"Not often; but sometimes, as in the present instance, it seems desirable. You see, our friends of the highway wouldn't be very apt to show themselves, if they should see a man with you."

"I don't know," said Andy, doubtfully. "Both of them together would be more than a match for us."

"You think so?" returned the detective. "I see you haven't a very high opinion of my abilities or physical strength."

"Hogan, as you call him, looks like a very strong man," said Andy.

"And I don't, eh?"

"Well," said Andy, not willing to give offense, "he is a good deal larger than you."

"That is true. But a man's strength isn't always in proportion to his size. Give me your hand, please."

Andy did so, though he did not quite understand the detective's object in making the request.

Perkins' hands were incased in tight-fitting

kid gloves, and were small for a man. What was Andy's surprise, then, to find his fingers in an ironlike grip that positively pained him. Perkins smiled as he felt Andy wince under the pressure.

"You've got the strongest hand of any lady I ever met," said Andy, with a smile.

"Suppose I get a grip on Mike Hogan?" suggested Perkins.

"I think he would find it hard to get away."

"He is the man I want. The other is of little consequence, compared with Hogan. If I can take but one, I shall hold on to the older villain."

As they traveled over the road, Perkins entertained his young companion with scraps of personal adventure, borrowed from his ten years' experience as a detective. He closed by instructing Andy how to act if they should encounter the men whom they sought.

Meanwhile, Hogan and the young man he called Bill, had stationed themselves near the road, in the shelter of some underbrush. Of the two, Hogan was the more excited and eager. His companion, under the impression that there was no money to be got from Andy, did not feel much interested in the mattter. True, Andy had played a trick upon him, but, although provoked, he rather applauded the boy's smartness.

With Mike Hogan it was different. He had

suffered physical pain at Andy's hands, besides losing, through his brave defense, the large sum which would otherwise unquestionably have fallen into his hands, and it was natural that he should thirst for revenge.

"I should like to wring the boy's neck," he muttered, as they lay together in concealment.

"It might not be altogether safe to kill him," suggested Bill, who shrank from murder, and feared that Hogan's temper might involve them in serious trouble.

"Oh, I won't kill him!" growled Hogan. "I wouldn't mind doing it, but for the law; but I don't want my neck stretched."

"That wouldn't pay, Hogan, as you say."

"I won't kill him, but I'll give him something to remember me by."

"That's all right; but don't go too far."

"I won't do any worse by him that he did by me, I tell you. Are you sure there is no other road, Bill, by which he can come back? I should feel like a fool if he went another way, while we were lying in wait for him."

"No danger, Hogan. I found out about that before I started."

Presently their waiting was rewarded. The sound of carriage wheels was heard.

"Look out and see who it is, Bill," said Hogan.

Bill peered through the leaves, looking cautiously up the road.

"It's the boy," he reported to his chief; "but he is not alone."

"Confusion!" muttered Mike Hogan, disappointed. "Who is with him?" he asked.

"Only a woman."

"Why didn't you say so before, you fool?" exclaimed Hogan, with an air of relief. "That won't make any difference."

"She'll scream!"

"Let her scream. No harm shall come to her. As for the boy, I'll attend to his case."

"What do you want me to do, Hogan?"

"Stop the horse, and I'll attend to the passengers."

By direction of Perkins, Andy drove a little slower when he came to the lonely part of the road.

"We'll give the gentleman a chance to stop us, my boy," said the detective.

The slow speed satisfied Hogan and his companion that Andy did not apprehend any attack, and that he would be all the more surprised and disconcerted when confronted by them.

According to the plan they had agreed upon, Bill jumped from the covert, and, dashing across the road, seized the horse by the head, while Mike Hogan, big and burly, with a menacing air, approached the wagon.

"Do you know me, young bantam?" he demanded, grimly.

" I think I've seen you before," said Andy, not seeming so much frightened as the thief expected.

" Yes, curse you! and I've seen you. You played a scurvy trick upon me Saturday night."

" I couldn't help it," said Andy. " I didn't want to hurt you, but you drove me to it."

" So, so! Well, it was unlucky for you, for I'm going to take pay out of your hide."

" What do you mean? " asked Andy, appearing disturbed.

" I am going to give you the worst thrashing you ever received."

" Pray don't! " entreated Andy. " Don't you see I have a lady here? Let me carry her home first."

" Do you think I am a fool? Get down, I say! "

" Then help the lady down first. She won't dare to stay in the carriage alone."

Mike Hogan had taken very little notice of the lady. At this request, he turned to her.

" Get down, ma'am, if you want to," he said. " I've got a score to settle with this young whelp."

Perkins took his hand lightly, and leaped to the ground.

The next moment he felt an iron grip at his collar, while the supposed lady held a revolver to his head.

" What does this mean? " he exclaimed, in utter amazement, recoiling from his fair companion.

With his unoccupied hand the detective threw back the veil which concealed his face.

" Mike Hogan," he said, " I've caught you at last."

" Who are you? " gasped the tramp and burglar.

" I am Perkins, the detective! "

It was a name that Mike Hogan knew well, though Andy had never heard of it. He started to tear himself away, but the iron grip was not disturbed.

" Surrender, or it will be all over with you," exclaimed Perkins, sternly.

Mike Hogan turned for help to his companion, but at the dreaded name Bill had escaped into the woods.

" I surrender," said the tramp, doggedly.

With Andy's help, handcuffs were put on the captive, and he was hoisted into the back part of the buggy. The horse's head was turned, and Andy drove back to Cranston, where there was a jail.

I may as well add here that Hogan was duly tried, and sentenced to a term of years in the State's prison.

Thus it happened that Andy was considerably later than he anticipated when he reached Hamilton on his return. During his absence his mother had received a letter which was of considerable importance.

CHAPTER XXII.

AN IMPORTANT PROPOSAL.

WHEN Mrs. Gordon heard of Andy's adventures during his ride to and from Cranston, she was naturally frightened.

" Oh, Andy! " she said, " I can't consent to your exposing yourself to be injured by such wicked men. You must tell the Peabody girls you can't go to the bank for them again."

" I don't think there'll be any danger, mother, for we have caught the chief burglar, and the other man has run away."

" There may be more of them," said Mrs. Gordon, apprehensively.

" Bring them along! " replied Andy, smiling. " I am ready for them! "

" I hope we shall never have another of those terrible men visit our village! " said his mother, with a shudder.

" I don't know about that, mother. . I find it pays me. How much do you think the Peabodys are going to give me for my services? "

" Perhaps two dollars," said Mrs. Gordon, looking at Andy in an inquiring way.

" Do you think two dollars would be pay enough for what I did, mother? "

" No; but boys are not paid as much as men, even where they are entitled to it."

" There's nothing mean about the Peabodys, mother. They have promised me more than that."

" Five dollars, perhaps."

" You will have to multiply five by ten!" said Andy, triumphantly.

" You don't mean to say you are to have fifty dollars?" ejaculated Mrs. Gordon, quite over-powered by surprise.

" Yes, I do. Toward night I'll go up and get the money. I didn't want to take it along to the bank, for I might have had that stolen, too."

" Certainly you are in luck, Andy," said his mother. " With what came in your poor father's wallet, we shall be very well off."

" Especially as we shall not have old Starr's note to pay. When do you expect the note to be presented?"

" Mr. Ross gave me a week to find the receipt."

" And the week will be up to-morrow. Well, mother, we will be ready for him when he comes."

At this moment Andy espied a letter on the mantelpiece. It was inclosed in a yellow en-velope, and addressed in an irregular, trem-ulous handwriting to his mother.

" What letter is that, mother?" he asked.

"I declare, Andy, I forgot to open it! Louis Schick brought it in an hour ago. He saw it at the post office, and knew you were away, so he brought it along."

"Why didn't you open it, mother? I thought ladies were always curious."

"I was mixing bread at the time, and my hands were all over dough, so I asked Louis to put it on the mantelpiece. When I got through with the bread I had forgotten all about the letter. I don't know when I should have thought of it again if you hadn't asked about it."

"You'd better open it, mother. Of course boys are never curious. Still, I should like to know what is in it. It may be money, you know."

From her work-basket Mrs. Gordon took a pair of scissors, and with them cut open the envelope. She drew out the letter, when, to the amazement of Andy and herself, a bank-note slipped out and fell upon the carpet.

"There is money inside, mother!" exclaimed our young hero, in surprise.

"How much is it?" asked his mother.

Andy stooped over and picked up the bank-note.

"Why, mother, it's a fifty-dollar bill!" he exclaimed. "It looks genuine, too. There's no humbug about it. Who can have sent us so much money?"

Meanwhile, Mrs. Gordon had been looking to the end of the letter to discover who had written it.

"Andy," she said, "it's from an old uncle of mine, who lives near Buffalo, in the town of Cato."

"What's his name, mother?"

"Simon Dodge. He is the oldest brother of my mother."

"You never mentioned him to me," said Andy.

"No; he had almost passed out of my recollection. Uncle Simon never wrote letters, and so it happens that, for twenty-five years, none of us have ever heard anything of him."

"Read his letter, mother. Let us hear what the fifty dollars are for. Perhaps he wants you to lay it out for him."

Mrs. Gordon began to read:

"MY DEAR NIECE: It is so long since you have heard from me, that you may have forgotten you had an uncle Simon. I never cared for letter writing—thought, from time to time, I have wished that I could hear something of you and how you were prospering. It is only with difficulty I have learned your address and gleaned a little knowledge of you.

"The way it happened was this: I met, last week, a peddler who had been traveling in your neighborhood. He had visited Hamilton, and I found he knew something about you. He told me that you were poor, and that your good husband was dead, but that you were blessed in having a fine boy to be a help and comfort to you."

Andy blushed when his mother read these words, and looked rather uncomfortable, as modest boys generally do when they hear themselves praised.

"As for me," the letter proceeded, "I am getting to be an old man. I am seventy-five years old, and, though my health is good and our family is long-lived—my father lived to be eighty-four—I feel that I have not long to live. I have had the good fortune to accumulate considerable property, besides the farm upon which I am living; but in spite of this, I find myself in a very uncomfortable position. I must explain to you how this happens.

"I had an only daughter—Sarah—who was everything that a daughter should be. She was amiable and kind, and, if she were living, I should have no cause to complain.

"She married a man named Brackett, a painter by trade, and for a few years they lived in a small house in the village. But Brackett was a lazy and shiftless man, and every year I had to help him, till at last I thought it would be cheaper taking him into my house and letting him help me look after the farm. My wife had died and I was willing to tolerate him—though I never liked the man —for the sake of my daughter's presence in the house. Five years afterward, Sarah died, but Brackett still remained. They had had no child that lived, and I should have liked then to have gotten rid of him, but it wasn't easy.

"Two years later he married a sharp, ill-tempered woman, from the next town, and brought her to the house. That was ten years ago. I ought to have given him notice to quit, but at the time of the marriage I was sick, and when I got well the new wife seemed to have become the mistress of the establishment.

"I have never been comfortable since. There are four children by this marriage, and they overrun the house. I was weak enough, a few years ago, to make over the place to Brackett, and now he and his wife are persecuting me to make a will, bequeathing them the rest of my property. This I will never do. The man has no claim upon me, and I should not have given him the place. My other property amounts to about ten thousand dollars, though he doesn't suspect it. I find myself watched, as a cat watches a mouse, lest I should dispose of my property away from them. I feel that I have not a friend in the house, and I am so old that I want one.

"Now, my dear niece, will you do me a favor? Send your boy to me, but let him take another name. I don't want it known or suspected that he is related to me. Though he is young, he can help me to carry out a plan I have in view, and to baffle my persecutors. I will take care that his services are recompensed. I enclose a fifty-dollar bill to pay his expenses out here.

"I am tired, and must close.

"Your old uncle,

"SIMON DODGE.

"P. S.—It will be a good idea to apply to Mr. Brackett for work—offering to come at very low wages. Brackett wants a boy, but he doesn't want to pay more than fifty cents a week. Do not answer this letter, if you send your son, as Mr. Brackett would find out that I had received a letter from your neighborhood, and his suspicions would be aroused."

CHAPTER XXIII.

ANDY'S RESOLVE.

"POOR uncle Simon!" said Mrs. Gordon, after the letter had been read. "He seems to be in a difficult position."

"Why doesn't he send that man Brackett packing?" asked Andy, indignantly. "He can't have much spirit."

"You forget, Andy, how old he is. An old man is not so well able to contend for his rights as a man of middle age. Besides, it appears that his son-in-law has possession of the farm."

"It is a shame!"

"So it is; but that cannot be recalled. The

rest of the property ought to be saved from Mr. Brackett."

"That's easy enough.   He needn't give it to him."

"But uncle Simon may be persecuted into doing what he does not wish to do."

"Mother," said Andy, with a sudden thought, "who will get the property if Mr. Dodge dies without a will?"

"I suppose it would go to his relations."

"What other relations has he besides you?"

"I don't think he has any others," answered Mrs. Gordon.

"Then it may come to us."

"We have more right to it than Mr. Brackett," said his mother.

"Then," said Andy, after a short pause, "there must be a struggle between me and Brackett."

"You wouldn't fight with a full-grown man, Andy?" asked his mother, in alarm.

"Oh, no!" answered Andy, smiling.   "I don't think it will come to that.   But I must go out to your uncle's help.   Between us both, we will see if we can't circumvent that grasping old Brackett and his wife and children."

"I don't see what a boy like you can do, Andy."

"At any rate, I can try, mother.   This money will pay my expenses out to Cato. When I get there I can form my plans."

"I don't see how I can spare you, Andy."

" Remember, mother, I am going in your behalf. Uncle Simon's money, which may
amount to ten thousand dollars, may otherwise
be taken from us."

" If you can induce Uncle Simon to come
here and end his days with us, I will try to
make him comfortable."

" A good idea, mother. I'll see if I can't
bring him."

" When do you want to start, Andy? "

" Not till after our good friend Joshua
Starr has come for his money. I want to be
here then, just to see how disappointed and
mortified he will look when he sees the receipt
with his signature attached."

On Tuesday afternoon, Joshua Starr called
at the office of Brandon Ross, the lawyer.

" To-day's the day when we are to call on
the Widder Gordon for my money, lawyer, isn't
it? " he said.

" Yes, Mr. Starr. Do you propose to come
with me? "

" Yes."

" It isn't necessary."

" You see, Squire, I thought I could take a
look at the furniture," suggested old Joshua,
" and decide what I'll take. It ain't likely that
the widder'll have the money to pay the note—
at least, not all of it, and I'll have to take it
out in what she's got."

" You are a hard man, Mr. Starr. I

shouldn't like to be owing you money which I couldn't pay."

"You're jokin', squire. There ain't anything wrong in my wantin' my money, is there?"

"No; still you're a rich man, and Mrs. Gordon is a poor woman."

"That ain't neither here nor there," said Joshua Starr, evidently annoyed. "My money's my own, I take it, and I'm entitled to it. If Mr. Gordon borrowed money, it stands to reason that his widder ought to pay it," he concluded, triumphantly.

"I can't gainsay you, Mr. Starr. You must act your will. I am only your agent, you know."

"Jes' so! jes' so!" said the old man, considerably relieved, for he feared that the lawyer was going to act against him.

But he did not know that Brandon Ross derived positive pleasure from the thought of the distress and trouble he was about to bring on the boy who had—as he construed it—insulted and injured his own spoiled son.

The crafty lawyer, however, did not mean to let either his client or his intended victim know how willingly he engaged in the affair.

CHAPTER XXIV.

ANDY'S TRIUMPH OVER MR. STARR.

"THEY'RE coming, mother," said Andy, as, looking from the window, he espied the bent form of old Joshua, with the sprucely dressed lawyer at his side, coming up the village street side by side, and approaching their modest cottage.

"I wish the visit were over," said Mrs. Gordon, nervously.

"I don't, mother," said Andy, with a smile of assured triumph. "The victory is to be ours, you know."

"I don't like to quarrel."

"Nor I; but when a man tries to impose upon me, I like to resist him boldly."

"You won't be too hasty, Andy?"

"No; but, mother, let me manage the matter, and leave me to produce the receipt when I think it best."

"Wouldn't it be well to save trouble by letting them know at once that we have found it, Andy?" asked the widow.

"No, mother; I want to make them show their hand first."

Andy had hardly completed this sentence, when a knock was heard at the door.

Mrs. Gordon opened it.

"Good-afternoon, widder!" said Joshua

Starr, in his cracked voice, which was usually pitched on a high key.

"Good-afternoon, Mrs. Gordon!" said the lawyer, blandly. "We have called—Mr. Starr and myself—on a little matter of business."

"Yes, ma'am, we've called on business," echoed Starr.

"Won't you walk in, gentlemen?" said Mrs. Gordon, gravely.

"Thank you!" said the lawyer.

And he bowed ceremoniously.

"I reckon we will," said Joshua Starr, who forgot to remove his battered old hat as he entered.

"Why, Andy, howdy do?" said the old man, as he espied our young hero seated at the window. "I see you've took to scarin' bur-glars. Ho, ho! I reckon I'd have to send for you if I had anything in my house wuth stealin'. Ho, ho!"

"Yes, Mr. Starr, I'm ready to defend myself against all sorts of burglars," said Andy, pointedly.

Mr. Starr did not understand Andy's mean-ing, but Mr. Ross darted a sharp glance at the boy, whom he understood better. He said nothing, however.

"Sho! I guess they ain't likely to get into your house, widder," said Mr. Starr, turning to Mrs. Gordon.

"I hope not, Mr. Starr."

The old man's eyes had already begun to wander about the room, in search of desirable furniture to seize in payment of the note. There was a comfortable rocking-chair, in which the lawyer had seated himself, which he mentally decided to claim. It occurred to him that it would be just the thing for him to sit in after the farm work of the day was over.

He nodded significantly to the lawyer, who thereupon commenced:

"Of course, Mrs. Gordon, you are aware of the nature of the business that has brought us here?"

"Jes' so! jes' so!" interjected Mr. Starr.

"Is it about the note?"

"Yes, it is about the note. Including interest, it amounts to——"

"One hundred and thirty-two dollars and twenty-seven cents," interrupted Joshua Starr, eagerly.

The lawyer looked at him angrily, and Mr. Starr shrank back in his chair.

"I told you, Mr. Ross, that the note had been paid," said Mrs. Gordon, beginning to be a little nervous.

"I know you said so," the lawyer returned, "and you were doubtless under that impression, but my client, Mr. Starr, assures me that it is a mistake. The note still remains unpaid."

"Jes' so! jes' so!" said Starr, eagerly.

"You know better, Mr. Starr!" broke in Andy, hotly. "You are trying to get the note paid twice."

"Why, Andy," exclaimed Mr. Starr, appearing to be very much shocked, "how you talk!"

"Young man," said the lawyer, severely, "this is very disgraceful! I cannot permit my respected client to be insulted by a beardless boy."

"What I said is true, nevertheless," said Andy. "I don't believe Mr. Starr has forgotten it, either!"

"That's all nonsense, Andy," said Joshua. "I'll make it easy for you. I'm willin' to take part of my pay in furniture, and the rest your mother can pay, say five or ten dollars a month."

"My mother has no more furniture than she wants," said Andy, "and she wants all her income to live upon."

"That won't do," said the lawyer, sternly. "Your mother must make some arrangements this very afternoon to pay my client's note, or it will be necessary for me, in his behalf, to take some very unpleasant measures."

"There is one excellent reason for our not paying the note," said Andy, smiling.

"What is that?"

"It has already been paid, and we can show Mr. Starr's receipt."

Mr. Ross and his client stared at each other

in a dismay which they were powerless to conceal.

––––––––

CHAPTER XXV.

MR. STARR'S CRUSHING DEFEAT.

THE old man, his mouth wide open in astonishment and dismay, presented a ludicrous spectacle. At first he seemed to be incapable of speech, but he managed to ejaculate, feebly:

" 'Tain't so—'tain't so ! "

" You will find that it is so, Mr. Starr," said Andy, firmly, " and that your wicked attempt to cheat my mother out of more than a hundred dollars has failed."

" I don't believe it," said Joshua Starr, nervously; but his voice showed that he did believe it, nevertheless.

He had the best reason for knowing that such a receipt had been signed, but he had reckoned on its being lost or permanently mislaid.

The lawyer was not sure in his own mind whether Andy was not deceiving them, and determined to find out.

" These are bold words, boy," he said. " We shall not believe in this receipt you talk about till you show it."

" Mr. Starr believes in it," retorted Andy, " for he knows very well he signed it; but he thought it was lost."

"I demand to see the receipt," said the lawyer.

"Very well; you shall see it," assented Andy.

He drew a wallet from his pocket, and, taking out a folded piece of paper, handed it to the lawyer.

"Let me see it," said Mr. Starr; but there was a cunning look in his eyes which made Andy distrustful.

"I object to his taking it," interposed our hero.

"I don't believe it's genewine," whined old Joshua. "It's a base attempt to cheat me out of my money."

"You'd better not talk about that, Mr. Starr," said Andy.

"Lemme see it."

"He has a right to see it," said Mr. Ross; but he spoke in a quiet tone, for he saw that it would injure his professional reputation to involve himself in an evident attempt at swindling.

Joshua Starr took the paper in his hand, and gazed at it in a dazed way.

"The signatoor don't look genewine," he said, weakly.

Now it chanced that Mr. Starr's signature was very peculiar—remarkable chiefly for its being a miserable scrawl.

"Doesn't it look like your writing?" said Andy.

"Well, mebbe it is, a little; but I guess it's a forgery. I dunno but you wrote it yourself, Andy."

"Do you believe that, Mr. Ross?" asked Andy, plainly.

"No," said the lawyer, with a glance of contempt at his client. "I believe it is Mr. Starr's signature."

Old Joshua's lower jaw dropped.

"You ain't a-goin' to desert me, squire, are you?"

As he spoke, he cunningly let go the receipt, giving it an impulse toward the open fireplace, where a fire was burning.

Andy, however, was on the watch, and he sprang forward and rescued the valuable document.

"What are you trying to do, Mr. Starr?" he demanded, sternly.

"Nothing—it slipped," answered the old man, crestfallen.

Though Mr. Ross was disappointed that he was unable to injure the Gordons by the agency of Mr. Starr, he felt that he could not afford to be implicated in the rascality which his client had attempted in his presence.

"Mrs. Gordon," he said, rising from his chair, "you will do me the justice to believe that I had no knowledge of the existence of this receipt. I supposed Mr. Starr's claim was a genuine one, or I would not have meddled with

it. It is not my intention to aid and abet
rascality."

" You don't mean me, do you, squire? " asked
Joshua Starr, gazing in consternation at the
lawyer.

" Yes, I do! " returned the lawyer, severely.

" There's a mistake, squire. I'm almost sure
that signatoor ain't genewine."

" And I am sure that it is," said the lawyer,
curtly. " You needn't bring me any more of
your business, Mr. Starr."

He strode out of the cottage, with a look of
utter disgust on his face.

" I don't see what's the matter with the
squire," said the old man. " He hadn't ought
to leave me that way."

" Have you got any more business with us,
Mr. Starr? " asked Andy.

" No—not as I know on. It's pretty hard
for me to lose all that money."

" You can try to cheat somebody else out of
it," said Andy, coolly. " I wouldn't advise
you to try us again."

" You're a cur'us boy, Andy," said the old
man, as he slowly rose and hobbled off, disappointed.

When Mr. Ross reached home, he found his
son Herbert waiting eagerly to interview him.

Herbert knew that his father had set out
with Mr. Starr for Andy Gordon's cottage,
and he was anxious to hear just what passed,

and whether Andy wasn't mortified and distressed.

"You've got back, pa?" said Herbert, by way of opening the conversation.

"Yes, I've got back!" said Mr. Ross, gruffly.

"I suppose Andy wasn't very glad to see you?" chuckled Herbert.

"It didn't seem to trouble him much," said the lawyer, curtly.

"He wasn't ready to pay the note, was he?" asked Herbert, in alarm.

"No."

Herbert felt relieved.

"I thought he couldn't raise the money," he said, triumphantly. "It was over a hundred dollars, wasn't it?"

The lawyer had been so much annoyed that he enjoyed the disappointment in store for his son, on the principle that misery loves company.

"There was no need of his having any money ready," he said.

"Mr. Starr hasn't excused him from paying it, has he?" inquired Herbert, anxiously.

"Mr. Starr is an old scoundrel!" exclaimed Mr. Ross, impetuously.

Herbert was petrified with astonishment at hearing his father speak thus of his client.

"Do you really mean it?" he asked, incredulously.

"Yes, I mean it."

" What has he done? "

" The note had been paid years ago, and he wanted to get it paid over again, and asked me to help him," said the lawyer, with virtuous indignation.

" Then he can't collect pay? " asked Herbert.

" Of course he can't. How many times do you think a man is bound to pay a note? "

Herbert was not pleased with the way things had turned out, and he was puzzled at the remarkable change which had taken place in his father.

" Then I suppose," he said, " you won't get anything for what you have done in the matter? "

The lawyer's eyes flashed. Here, at least, was a chance to get even with the old cheat, as he now denominated Mr. Starr. The next morning he sent a bill to Joshua Starr for professional services, setting the sum at fifteen dollars. This quickly brought the old man around to his office, in terrible dismay.

" You ain't in earnest, squire? " he said.

" About what? "

" About this bill."

" Mr. Starr, do you suppose I work for nothing? "

" But you didn't collect any money for me, squire."

" And whose fault was that, I'd like to

know?" retorted the lawyer. "It appears that your claim was fraudulent—fraudulent, Mr. Starr!"

Mr. Joshua Starr cared very little about the damage to his reputation arising from detection in such a dirty trick, but he cared a great deal about the fifteen dollars.

"It ain't right for you to ask it, squire. You didn't do me a mite of good."

"What business had you to obtain my help in such a scandalous fraud?"

"Suppose we call it even, squire. You ain't succeeded, and——"

"I shall succeed in this, Mr. Starr. That bill must be paid."

"I won't pay it!" said the old man, obdurately.

"You won't, eh? Then I'll attach your farm."

Finally Joshua Starr had to pay the lawyer's charge, and I think the verdict of my young readers will be: "Served him right."

Two days afterward, to the astonishment of every one except his mother and Dr. Euclid, whom he took into his confidence, Andy Gordon left Hamilton, and was not seen in the village again for several weeks.

Where he went, and what he did, will be explained in succeeding chapters.

CHAPTER XXVI.

ANDY'S NEW NAME.

ANDY had to consider what name he would assume in place of his own.

His mother did not like the idea of his changing his name.

" It looks as if you had something to be ashamed of," she said.

" But I haven't, mother."

" Generally, only criminals who are engaged in breaking the laws change their names," persisted Mrs. Gordon.

" Do you think, mother," laughed Andy, " that changing my name will make me a law-breaker? "

" No, Andy; but——"

" But, mother, it seems to be necessary. That man Brackett knows that uncle Simon has relations, and it is likely that he knows our name.　If I should appear as Andy Gordon he would know the name, and be suspicious of me, so that I could not help uncle at all."

Mrs. Gordon had to admit that Andy was right.

" I suppose it must be, then," she said. " What name have you thought of? "

" I have not thought of any yet, but it can't be very hard to find one.　Names are plenty enough."

This was true.　Still, after suggesting a

dozen, Andy seemed no nearer a choice than he had been in the first place.

"I'll tell you what, mother," he said at last. "Haven't you an old paper here, somewhere?"

One was found.

"I am going to find a name somewhere in this paper," said Andy, and forthwith he began to examine critically the crowded columns.

He paused at a paragraph, recording the bravery of a boy named Henry Miller, who had saved a younger boy from drowning, somewhere in Massachusetts. This struck Andy favorably.

"Mother," he said, "let me introduce myself to you as Henry Miller."

"Do you like the name?" asked his mother, doubtfully.

"Not particularly, but it is the name of a brave boy, and so is an honorable name. I shouldn't like a bad name, like Benedict Arnold, for instance."

"What did Henry Miller do?"

"He saved a boy from drowning."

So it was decided that Andy, as soon as he left Hamilton, should be known as Henry Miller.

He had, as we know, intended to buy a new suit of clothes, but as he was about to assume the character of a poor boy, wandering about the country in search of employment, that would hardly be worth while.

He decided to wear his everyday clothes, and carry his best in a bundle, with some necessary underclothing.

Andy found on inquiry that the town of Cato, where his great-uncle lived, was nearly four hundred miles distant.

Of course, there would be no occasion to assume his character till he got nearly there.

From a railroad guide he ascertained the name of a place about fifteen miles from Cato, and bought a ticket to that place.

We will call this place Seneca, though that was not the name.

Before leaving Hamilton it was not only proper but incumbent on Andy to call on Dr. Euclid, and resign his post as janitor.

" Going to leave us, Andrew? " said the doctor, in a tone of regret. " I am sorry to hear it. Can't you stay till the end of the term? "

" No, sir; I shall have to go at once," answered Andy.

" If it is any money embarrassment," said the doctor, kindly, " don't let that influence you. I shall be very glad to assist you, if you will allow me."

Dr. Euclid spoke in a tone of kindness and delicate sympathy which could hardly have been expected of the stern master at whose frown so many boys trembled.

Andy was exceedingly grateful, and felt that he ought to say so.

" Thank you for your great kindness, Dr. Euclid," said Andy; " but it isn't that—though it does relate to money. Though it is a secret, I have a great mind to tell you."

" Do as you please, Andrew. I shall, of course, respect your confidence, and perhaps I may be able to advise you for your benefit."

Upon this, Andy told the doctor the whole story, reading him his uncle's letter, which he happened to have in his pocket.

" It is a serious undertaking, my boy," said the doctor. " Do you think you are equal to it? "

" I may be self-conceited, Dr. Euclid, but I think I am," answered Andy.

" I would not call it self-conceit," said the doctor, slowly, " but a spirit of confidence which may be justified by events. Have you any plan of proceedings? "

" No, sir; except to follow uncle Simon's instructions, and try to get a place in Mr. Brackett's employ, where I can be ready to be of service."

" I suspect you won't find the place an easy one. Probably this Mr. Brackett will make you work hard."

" I am afraid so," laughed Andy; " but I will remember that I am working for a higher reward than the fifty cents a week which uncle writes that I may be paid."

" On the whole," said the doctor, " I think

you are acting right. You have a good end in view, and, what is very important, you are leaving home with your mother's knowledge and with her permission. Were it otherwise, I should think you were acting decidedly wrong."

"I should not think of leaving home without mother's permission," said Andy, promptly.

"Quite right, my boy," said the doctor, kindly. "I am sorry to say that in these days of juvenile independence not all boys are so considerate. Well, Andrew, you have my best wishes for your success. I hope we may soon see you home again, and your uncle with you."

"That is what I shall try for," answered Andy. "I would like to get him out of the clutches of that man Brackett."

On his way home, Andy did not take the most direct route, but, crossing the fields, walked along the shores of Brewster's Pond— a sheet of water only half a mile across, but quite deep in parts.

As he reached the shore of the pond, he heard a scream, and, quickly looking round, saw a boat, bottom up, and a boy clinging desperately to it. The boat was only a hundred and fifty feet away.

Andy was an expert swimmer, and he did not hesitate a moment. Throwing off his coat, he plunged into the water and swam out to the boat with a strong and sturdy stroke.

He reached the boy just in time, for he was

about to let go his hold, his strength having been overtaxed.

Then, for the first time, Andy saw that the boy whom he was attempting to rescue was Herbert Ross.

" Rest your hand on my shoulder, Herbert," he said, " but don't grasp me so that I can't swim."

Herbert gladly obeyed instructions, and, with some difficulty, Andy helped him to land.

" Now, Herbert, go home at once, or you will catch your death of cold," said Andy.

" I'm much obliged to you," replied Herbert, shivering. " Here, take that."

Andy could hardly believe his eyes when the boy, whose life he had saved, offered him a twenty-five cent piece.

" No, thank you!" he said, smiling. " I don't need any reward."

" I would rather you would take it."

" It is quite impossible," said Andy, shortly. " I advise you to go home as fast as you can."

" What a mean boy!" exclaimed Mrs. Gordon, when Andy, who came home wet through, told her of the munificent sum offered him.

" I don't know," said Andy, smiling. " Herbert understands best the value of his own life. But, mother, now that this has happened, I shall feel quite justified in taking the name of Henry Miller, for I, too, have saved a boy from drowning."

The next day he started on his journey.

CHAPTER XXVII.

ANDY MEETS HIS PREDECESSOR.

IT was a bright, pleasant morning when Andy left Seneca for the town of Cato, where his great-uncle lived. He had arrived in Seneca the evening previous, and passed the night at the village inn, where he had obtained two meals and lodging for seventy-five cents.

"Where be you going?" asked the landlord —a stout and good-natured looking man.

"I guess I'll travel a little further," said Andy, smiling.

For obvious reasons he did not like to say he was going to Cato, as the inquisitive landlord would undoubtedly ask him why.

"Ain't you got no folks?"

"I have no wife and family," said Andy, laughing.

"Sho, that isn't what I mean! Isn't your father or mother living?"

"Yes; I have a mother."

"Where does she live?"

"Down East."

"I s'pose you're seeking your fortune, ain't you?"

"A little of that," said Andy; "but, you see, I like to travel."

"I'll tell you what I'll do. You seem a spry, active boy. If you'll stay here and make yourself useful about the house and stable,

I'll give you all you can eat and five dollars a month. Now, what do you say?"

"I wouldn't mind working for you," said Andy, "only I want to travel a little further."

"'A rolling stone gathers no moss,' as the schoolmaster says."

"That is true. But, you see, I am not ready to settle down yet. I'm much obliged to you for you kind offer!"

"You talk as if you'd got money. A boy like you wouldn't give up a good place if he didn't see his way clear enough to eat."

"I'm not very rich, Mr. Jenkins, but I am not afraid of starving. Perhaps I will stop on my way back."

"That's right; but you'd better stay now."

"On the whole," thought Andy, "I think I could get something to do if I needed it. I have no doubt I should find the good-natured landlord a pleasanter man to work for than Mr. Brackett; but I must not forget my errand."

So Andy began to trudge along the road toward Cato. It was rather a lonely road, with only here and there a house, but there were signboards, so that there was no danger of losing the way. Andy took it easy, now and then throwing himself down by the side of the road to rest.

"I've got all day before me," he reflected. "There's no need to hurry and use myself up."

So it happened that it took him four hours to accomplish ten miles. By this time he was quite hungry, and would have been glad to come across a hotel. There was none, however, short of Cato, and Andy didn't think he could wait till then before satisfying his hunger.

It was at this point that he saw approaching him a boy, apparently about his own age, with a shock of bright red hair, a freckled face, and a suit of clothes of unknown antiquity. He, too, had a small bundle, put up in a red cotton handkerchief.

" Must be my twin brother! " thought Andy. " I'll speak to him."

The newcomer stared at Andy, but whether he would have spoken is not quite certain, if our hero had not taken the initiative.

" Good-morning, Johnny! " said Andy.

" My name ain't Johnny; it's Peter. Who be you? " returned the other.

" I'm a traveler, just at present," answered Andy.

" They calls 'em tramps round our way," said Peter.

" Then I suppose you're a tramp," said Andy.

" That's so, and I'm blest if I like it! "

" Where do you come from? "

" From Cato."

" Just what I wanted," thought Andy.   " He

can give me some information. Won't you sit down and rest a little while with me?"

"I dunno but I will. Where are you goin'?" asked Peter, his face expressing curiosity.

"What is the nearest place?"

"Cato."

"Then I guess I'll go there."

"I wouldn't."

"Don't you like the place?"

"The place is good enough; but I worked for an awful mean man."

"Who was it?" asked Andy, with a presentiment of what the answer might be.

"His name is Brackett. Ain't he mean, though? But his wife's jest as bad. Jaw, jaw, jaw, all the time! I couldn't stand it, so I left."

"That's encouraging," thought Andy. "Was there any one else in the family?"

"There was four children—reg'lar terrors! I'd like to choke 'em."

"Come, Peter, you're not in earnest?"

"Ain't I, though! They're the wust behaved youngsters I ever come across."

"I suppose there was no one else in the family?"

"Yes, there was an old gentleman—a nice old man, he was! I wouldn't have minded workin' for him. He always had a good word for me, but old Brackett and his wife was scoldin' all the time."

" What was the name of the old man? "

" Mr. Dodge.   I guess it's he that owns the property; but Lor'! he don't have anything to say about it. Brackett and his wife have things all their own way."

" How long were you working for Mr. Brackett? "

" About six weeks."

" I suppose he paid you well? "

" Paid me well!" repeated Peter, scornfully. " How much do you calc'late he paid me? "

" About two dollars a week," said Andy, demurely.

Peter burst into a scornful laugh.

" Much you know old Brackett, if you think he'd pay that figger," he said. " He paid me seventy-five cents a week, and kept groanin' over the big wages he was a-payin'! He wanted to get me for fifty cents! "

" He is certainly not a very generous man, Peter."

" No; I guess not."

" Did you save enough to retire on a fortune? " asked Andy, laughing.

Poor Peter looked sad.

" Blest if I've got more'n twenty-five cents in the world!" he said; "and I'm awful hungry."

" So am I, Peter. But I don't see any chance to get dinner, even if we had ever so much money."

"We could git some over yonder," said Peter, pointing to a farmhouse some way back from the road. "Only we might have to pay for it."

"Then come along," said Andy. "Let's go there."

Peter hung back.

"You see, I don't want to spend all my money," he said. "I ain't got but twenty-five cents."

"It shan't cost you a cent. I will pay for both our dinners."

"You will?" exclaimed Peter, gladly. "Have you got money enough?"

"Oh, yes, I've got enough for that."

"Then, come along!"

Five minutes later they were knocking at the door of the farmhouse.

A woman, who had evidently been busy getting dinner, her face being flushed with the heat of the kitchen stove, came to the door and surveyed the boys with suspicion.

"What do you want?" she asked.

"Madam," said Andy, pulling off his hat politely, "my friend and I are hungry, and——"

"We ain't got anything for tramps," said the woman, sourly.

"But," said Andy, in unfailing good humor, "we are not what you suppose."

"You mean to say you ain't tramps? I'll

bet a ninepence that you'd steal the spoons, jest as soon as my back was turned."

Peter was about to return an angry answer, but Andy checked him.

"We don't want you to give us a dinner," he said; "but to sell us one. I have money and will pay you in advance if you like."

The woman—by the way, she was a close-fisted widow, who was always ready to turn a penny, but not to give even a penny's worth away—was surprised and incredulous.

"Have you any money?" she asked.

"To be sure! How much shall I pay you?" and Andy brought out his pocket-book.

"A quarter apiece, I reckon. I've only got sassidges and pie for dinner, but it ought to be wuth that."

Andy was not over fond of sausages, but the smell of them frying was particularly appetizing just then, and he very readily produced half a dollar and put it into the hands of the Widow Simpson.

"Step right in," said the widow, with sudden civility. "Dinner will be ready in a jiffy. Here, you Mary Ann, dish up them sassidges, and fry some more. There's two young gentlemen goin' to dine with us."

"We were tramps a minute ago," thought Andy, amused.

CHAPTER XXVIII.

ANDY ARRIVES IN CATO.

MARY ANN was an overgrown girl, with red arms and prominent knuckles, and no personal beauty to speak of. She was good-natured, however, and thus had an advantage over her mother.

She stared at the two guests as they sat up to the table, and was evidently favorably impressed by the appearance of Andy, who was a good-looking boy. Peter did not appear to please her so much, and merely received a look.

Mrs. Simpson was bustling about the kitchen and adjoining room, and left Mary Ann to entertain her guests. The girl showed her partiality for Andy by putting three sausages on his plate, and only two on Peter's; but the latter took no notice of the discrimination, but set to work at once on his share.

Mary Ann looked at Andy with what she meant to be an engaging smile, though it looked more like a broad grin.

" I hope you like the sassidges?" she said.

" They are very good, thank you," replied Andy, politely.

He spoke correctly, for Mrs. Simpson was famed for the excellence of her sausages, of which she annually made a large stock, part of which were sent to market.

"They was made out of one of our best hogs," said Mary Ann, with engaging frankness.

"I don't think I ever ate better," said Andy.

"They're hunky!" chimed in Peter, with his mouth full.

"Is you travelin' far?" asked Mary Ann, who was not very well versed in grammar.

"Not very," answered Andy.

"Be you a peddler?"

"No; but I may take up the business some time."

"If you ever do, be sure to call round and see us, whenever you come our way," said the young lady.

"I certainly will. I shan't forget your nice sausages."

"Won't you have another?" asked Mary Ann, looking pleased.

"No, thank you."

"I will," said Peter.

Mary Ann supplied his wants, though not with as good a grace as she would have done for his companion.

"I guess you'll have some pie?" she suggested, to Andy.

"Thank you."

A liberal slice of apple pie was put on his plate. Andy would have preferred a clean plate, as sausages and apple pie do not go well together, but he did not care to be so particular.

The pie was good, also, and our hero, whose appetite was of that kind sometimes described as "healthy," felt that he was getting his full money's worth. As for Peter, he ate as if he were ravenous, and, not being engaged in conversation, like Andy, was able to give his undivided attention to the subject in hand.

"How are you gettin' on, young men?" asked Mrs. Simpson, as she passed through the room.

"Bully!" mumbled Peter, whose utterance was somewhat impeded by the half section of apple pie which he had thrust into his mouth.

"Your daughter is taking excellent care of us," said Andy.

Mary Ann looked delighted at this tribute to her attention, and mentally pronounced Andy the handsomest and most polite boy she had ever chanced to meet.

"What is your name?" she inquired, by no means bashful.

"You may call me Henry Miller," said Andy, using his assumed name for the first time.

"That's a nice name," said Mary Ann.

"Do you think so?" asked Andy, smiling.

"I've got a nice name myself," said Peter, complacently.

"What's your name?" asked the young lady, indifferently.

"My name's Peter Jenks."

"I don't like it," said Mary Ann, decidedly, looking unfavorably at the red-headed boy.

"You wouldn't like to be Mrs. Jenks?" asked Peter, grinning.

"No, I wouldn't. I don't want to marry no red head."

"Maybe you'd like him better," said Peter, pointing to Andy. "I guess anybody would."

Andy was amused. He saw that he had made a conquest of the young lady, but did not feel much flattered. He would have been perfectly willing to transfer all her admiration to his companion, if the young lady had been willing.

When the dinner was over the two boys rose from the table, and, bidding good-by to Mary Ann and her mother, left the farmhouse.

"I say, that was a hunky dinner," said Peter.

"It was very good, indeed."

"It was enough sight better than I got at old Brackett's."

"Don't they live well there?"

"No, they don't. The old woman ain't much of a cook. Besides, she's mean. We didn't have pie, only now and then, and she'd cut a pie into eight pieces, and there wasn't no chance of a second slice for me."

"By the way, Peter," said Andy, with a sudden thought, "how would you like to work at a hotel?"

"First class!" answered Peter, promptly.

"Were you ever in Seneca?"

"Once."

"You know the way, then?"

"Yes; straight ahead."

"The landlord of the hotel there offered me a place, to work round the hotel and stable, for five dollars a month and board."

"Why didn't you take it?"

"I didn't care to, just now."

"I wish I could get it," said Peter, wistfully.

"I think you can. Go straight there, and tell the landlord you were sent to him by a boy you met on the road. He'll know it was I who sent you, and I shouldn't wonder if you'd get the place."

"I'll do it," said Peter, with a look of determination; "but I don't see why you don't go back and take it yourself?"

"Oh, I don't care for it," said Andy.

Peter would have been very much surprised had he known that Andy's reason for declining to enter the landlord's services was on account of his desire to step into the old place which he had just left with so much disgust.

"You must have a lot of money," he said.

"Oh, no," said Andy, laughing. "What makes you think so?"

"You wouldn't give up a good place if you hadn't."

"Haven't you given up your place, Peter?"

"Yes; but it wasn't a good one. I'm much obliged to you for the dinner you've given me."

"Oh, you are quite welcome. I suppose we part here. Of course you'll go right on to Seneca, while I trudge on to Cato."

"Yes," said Peter. "I'll try for that place before night."

"I hope you'll get it."

So the two boys parted, and Andy kept on. He felt considerably more comfortable now that he had eaten a hearty dinner, but did not feel like walking rapidly. There was plenty of time to get to Cato, for he was not over five miles away.

"I guess I'll go round to see Mr. Brackett to-night," thought our hero, "so as to reach him before he has had a chance to hire another boy. I expect, from Peter's account, I shan't have a very pleasant time, but I shall soon see how the land lies, and whether there is any chance of helping uncle Simon or not. If I don't get enough to eat, there's one comfort—I have money in my pocket, and I can buy something outside. Money's a pretty good friend, under all circumstances."

Arrived in the village, Andy walked slowly along the road, keeping his eyes wide open.

A little in advance of him he saw an old man, with white hair, who was walking slowly, and appeared rather feeble.

"I shouldn't be surprised if that is uncle Simon," he thought. "I'll speak to him, and try to find out."

CHAPTER XXIX.

SIMON DODGE.

ANDY quickened his pace until he found himself walking beside the old gentleman. He was in doubt how to address him, in order to ascertain whether it was really his mother's uncle. If he were not, he must be on his guard not to say anything which might excite the suspicions of any one as to his having a special purpose in visiting Cato. The way was made easy for him, however.

The old man was Simon Dodge, and he was in daily expectation of the appearance of his niece's son.

When he saw Andy, in his traveling garb, with his little bundle of clothes under his arm, his eyes lighted up with hope, and he immediately accosted him.

"Where are you traveling, my boy?" he asked, eagerly.

"I have come from the East," answered Andy. "I shall stay here, if I can find a place."

"Would you be willing to work on a farm?" asked the old man.

"Yes," answered our hero. "I hear that

there is a farmer named Brackett who wants to hire a boy. Do you know where he lives?"

"Yes—yes, I can tell you. I am Mr. Brackett's father-in-law," said the old man, quickly.

Andy looked about him cautiously, to make sure that no one could overhear him, and said, in a low voice:

"Then you are my mother's uncle—Mr. Dodge!"

The old man's face lighted up with satisfaction.

"So I thought," he answered. "I thought you were Mary's son as soon as I looked at you. My dear boy, I am glad, heartily glad, to see you!"

Andy looked up in the old man's face, and he saw there an expression of a kind and amiable disposition.

He could understand how such a man should have allowed himself to be imposed upon by a selfish and unscrupulous man like Brackett.

"I am glad to see you, Uncle Simon!" he said. "I hope I may be able to be of service to you."

"You seem like a strong, active boy," said the old man, surveying, with approval, the sturdy frame and manly, handsome features of his great-nephew.

"Yes," returned Andy, smiling, "I am tolerably strong."

"What is your name?"

" Andrew Gordon; they generally call me Andy."

" I should like to call you by that name, but it will be more prudent to go by some other."

" You may call me Henry Miller, Uncle Simon."

" Henry Miller? I will try to remember it. But you mustn't call me Uncle Simon; that would ruin all, if Mr. Brackett should hear it."

" I'll be cautious—never fear! Can you advise me how to act? Shall I call at the farm to-night? "

" Yes. Mr. Brackett is looking out for a boy. His boy left him this morning."

" I know it."

" You know it? " said the old man, in surprise. " How did you hear of it? "

" I met Peter on the road and treated him to a dinner."

" Indeed! What did he say about leaving? "

" He doesn't seem to be in love with Mr. Brackett," laughed Andy. " He says you are a nice old gentleman."

" Yes; Peter and I always got along well together."

" What sort of a boy is he? " asked Andy, with some curiosity.

" He's not a bad sort of boy; he liked to play now and then, but he is as good as the average. Mr. Brackett expects too much of boys."

" I suppose he will expect too much of me."

" I am afraid you won't like the place," said Mr. Dodge, anxiously. " But bear in mind, you shall have all the money you want, only Brackett mustn't know anything about it. We will have a secret understanding together, Andy—I mean Henry."

" Yes, sir. I wouldn't stay, if it were not for the sake of helping you."

" Thank you! It will make me feel better to think I have one friend in the house; only we must be cautious."

" Uncle Simon," said Andy, boldly, " why do you stay here with this man? My mother asked me to invite you to come back with me to Hamilton. Our house is small, but we can make room for you. You won't have anything to complain of there, and you can leave your money where you like. You won't have any hints from us."

Mr. Dodge's face lighted up with pleasure, and he asked eagerly:

" Will your mother be really willing to be trouble with me for the little time I have to stay on earth? "

" She will be glad to have you with us," answered Andy, emphatically. " If you were a man like Mr. Brackett—as I suppose he is— she wouldn't want you; but I am sure we shall find you a pleasant visitor."

" It is what has come into my mind, my boy," said the old man; " but I was afraid your mother wouldn't like it. I could ask nothing better. I am not happy where I am. Mr. and Mrs. Brackett are continually asking me for money and scheming to have me leave them what money I have left. Only this morning, Brackett was urging me to make a will, for he knows that, if I die, he is no relative of mine, and the law wouldn't give him the money."

" You have given him the farm already, haven't you, Uncle Simon? "

" Yes; and a good farm it is. I not only gave it to him, but I gave him the stock and tools, and all I asked in return was that I should receive my board."

" I don't think he has any right to complain."

" No, he has no right to complain; but he does complain. He pretends that the farm doesn't give him a living, and is always wanting to borrow money."

" Do you let him have it? "

" Sometimes. I cannot help it, he is so importunate."

" Does he ever pay you back? "

" Never! " said Mr. Dodge, emphatically. " He pretends he can't."

Andy looked the disgust he felt.

" Uncle Simon," he said, " you treat him altogether too well. I wouldn't give in to him that way."

" And I suppose you think I ought not to? "

" Yes, I do think so."

" Andy, you don't know what it is to be old
and weak. When a man gets to be seventy-
five," said Simon, in a pathetic voice, " he
doesn't want to be at strife. He wants peace
and rest. Twenty years ago, or even ten years
ago, I should have been better able to resist
Mr. Brackett; now he annoys and worries
me."

" How long has he been trying to get you to
make a will in his favor? "

" For at least two years."

" I almost wonder you didn't do it to get
rid of him."

" I will never do that," said Simon Dodge,
with an energy that surprised Andy. " It
wouldn't be safe," he added, lowering his
voice.

" Why wouldn't it be safe? " inquired our
hero, not without curiosity.

" I believe Brackett and his wife would take
care that they didn't have to wait long for
their money."

" You don't mean to say that they would
make away with you? " said Andy, startled.

" I hope not—I hope not. But I don't
think it safe to expose them to temptation,"
said Mr. Dodge, shaking his head.

They had been walking slowly. At a point
in the road, the prospect widened out before
them.

" That is where we live," said the old man,
pointing to a farmhouse, perhaps a quarter

of a mile away. "We had better separate here, for it is not best that Mr. Brackett should suppose there is any understanding or acquaintance between us. You might come round in about an hour and apply for a place. Be prepared to accept fifty cents a week."

"All right!"

And he sat down by the side of the road to rest, for he was really tired, while the old man bent his steps toward home.

CHAPTER XXX.

MR. JEREMIAH BRACKETT.

MR. BRACKETT, a loose-jointed, shambling figure of a man, was leaning against the well curb, smoking a pipe, when his wife appeared at the back door and called out:

"Jeremiah!"

"What's wanted?" asked Brackett, impatiently.

"I want some firewood, right off!"

"You're always wanting firewood!" grumbled her husband.

"I should like to know how you expect me to cook your supper without wood to burn," retorted Mrs. Brackett.

"Send out Tom for some."

Tom was the eldest of Mr. Brackett's children, and had now attained the age of eight years.

"So I have; and he says there isn't any

split," said Mrs. Brackett. "Just fly around and saw and split some, or I shall have the fire out."

Mr. Brackett took the pipe from his mouth and sauntered toward the wood pile in a very discontented frame of mind.

"My wife burns a sight of wood," he said to himself. "It's saw and split all the time. That's where I miss Peter. The lazy little vagabond, to leave me this morning, and now I've to do his work and my own, too."

Peter might be a lazy little vagabond, but the work he did was certainly more than fell to the lot of his employer, though he had worked for almost nothing.

The fact was, Mr. Brackett was a lazy man, and considered that in superintending others he was doing all that could be expected of him.

Peter had milked three of the six cows, foddered them, cleaned out the stalls, sawed and split the wood, and done the numberless chores Mrs. Brackett found for him, besides doing a share of the farmwork.

At times during the year, Mr. Brackett hired a man by the day, but generally had a quarrel with him when pay day came, being as mean as he was lazy.

Jeremiah Brackett began to ply the saw and ax, knowing that his supper depended upon it, and soon little Tommy was able to carry in an armful to his mother.

He sawed a little more, and then resumed his smoking.

" It's slave, slave all the time! " he muttered. " The old man might help me a little, now that I've lost Peter—but no, he's too much of a gentleman. He must take his cane and walk off for pleasure. I wish I had nothing else to do but to walk for pleasure."

It would have occurred to any one else that at the age of seventy-five a man might have been allowed to rest, particularly when his life up to seventy had been spent in active duty; but Mr. Brackett was intensely selfish and grudged his father-in-law his well-earned leisure.

He never seemed to think of the rich and productive farm, worth fully ten thousand dollars, which he had received from Mr. Dodge, and was disposed to think that in giving the old gentleman a room for it in his own house, with fare at a very meager table, he was really making a hard bargain.

" If the old man would only give me two thousand dollars in money," he reflected, " it would make me easy. Of course, it's coming to me some time—there isn't anybody else that has any claim—but it looks as if he meant to live forever."

Mr. Brackett did not, however, feel quite so sure of the personal property as he wished. He knew that Mr. Dodge had relations in Ham-

ilton, and it was the fear of his life that they
would inherit the coveted stocks and bonds.

He was somewhat reassured, however, by
the knowledge that his father-in-law never appeared to write or receive a letter.

Of the letter which had been received by
Mrs. Gordon, and led to the journey of our
young hero, he knew nothing. It would have
occasioned him a great amount of uneasiness
if he had heard anything of it.

He was still smoking when Simon Dodge,
fresh from his interview with Andy, entered
the yard.

"Been out walking, father?" asked Brackett.

He was careful never to let the old man forget the relationship which existed between
them, though, in truth, there was no relationship at all.

"Yes, Jeremiah, I must take a little exercise,
so as not to get stiff in the joints."

"I have plenty of exercise at home," grumbled Brackett. "I have had to attend to all
Peter's chores, in addition to my own work."

"Oh, well, you'll get another boy soon,"
said old Simon, cheerfully.

"I hope so, for I don't want to get worn
out. When a man has a wife and children to
support, he's got a tough job before him."

"Not when he's got a good farm like this,"
said Mr. Dodge.

" There ain't any money to be made by farming," muttered Brackett.

" That wasn't my experience," said Mr.
Dodge. " When I was twenty-five I inherited
this farm from my father; but there was a
debt of three thousand dollars on it, which I
was to pay my brother for his share. I hadn't
a cent outside. Well, I worked hard, and I
waited patiently, and in time I paid off the
mortgage I put on it to pay my brother, and
when I gave it up to you, it was in good condition and well stocked. You started a good
deal better off than I did."

" Some folks have more luck than others,"
said Brackett.

" If there was any difference in luck," said
the old man, dryly, " it was in your favor. It's
labor more than luck that counts in this world,
according to my thinking."

" You didn't have four children to support,
father."

" I had three, and while only one lived to
grow up, the other two lived to be older than
any of yours."

" I don't know how it is," said Brackett,
" but I'm always hard up. The children ought
to have new clothes, but where I am to get the
money I don't know."

Mr. Dodge did not offer to tell Mr. Brackett
where it was to be got, but he could have done
so.

Mrs. Brackett had five hundred dollars in

a savings-bank, which, in spite of his laziness, Brackett, with her help, had been able to save.

The two had decided that Mr. Dodge was on no account to know anything of this, as it might prevent his doing anything for them; but the old man had learned it indirectly; and the knowledge helped him to remain deaf to their application for assistance. So, when they pleaded poverty, he remained politely silent.

"Father," said Brackett, "will you lend me fifty dollars for six weeks, till I've had a chance to sell some of my grain?"

Mr. Dodge knew very well from repeated experience that there wasn't one chance in ten of any such loan being repaid to him. In fact, Brackett owed him, in the aggregate, nearly a thousand dollars, borrowed on just such conditions—to be repaid in six weeks.

"I think you must excuse me, Jeremiah," said Simon Dodge, quietly.

"It would set me on my feet," said Brackett.

As he leaned against the well curb in a languid attitude, it really seemed as if he needed somebody or something to set him on his feet.

"I think you will have to look for the money somewhere else," replied his father-in-law.

"I thought you was having some interest coming in at this time, father."

"Jeremiah, I gave you the farm, and with good management, you never need to borrow.

It ought to support you handsomely, as it did me. I have told you that more than once."

Simon Dodge left his son-in-law, and entered the house.

"How the old miser hangs on to his money!" growled Brackett. "He's getting more and more selfish and mean as he grows older. I wish he'd make his will. If he should die now, I'm afraid them Eastern relatives would be after the property."

Just then, however, his attention was drawn to a boy, with a bundle under his arm, who was entering the gate. It was Andy.

CHAPTER XXXI.

ANDY IS ENGAGED.

JEREMIAH BRACKETT brightened up as his glance took in the strong, sturdy figure of our hero.

He stood very little chance of securing the services of a boy belonging to the village, for his penurious disposition was too well known; but here was a stranger, who knew nothing about him, and who was probably in search of employment."

"Is this Mr. Brackett?" asked Andy, politely.

"Yes; that's my name."

"I was told you wanted to hire a boy."

"Who told you so?"

"A boy I met on the road."

"Was his name Peter?"

"I believe he said so."

"A lazy, shiftless boy!" said Brackett, warmly. "He had a good place here, and I looked after him as if he had been my own son; but he didn't do his duty."

"He didn't say anything about that," said Andy, gravely.

"No, I reckon not. Did he say anything about me?" asked Brackett.

"He said you and he couldn't get along very well."

"All his own fault," returned the farmer, who wished to remove any prejudice which Peter's story may have excited in the mind of Andy. "He had as nice a home as any boy would want, and easy work; but some boys are never satisfied. Was you looking for work?"

"I thought I might hire out for a while."

"What do you call yourself?"

"Henry Miller."

"Was you raised near here?"

"Not very."

"Did you ever work on a farm?"

"I have worked a little in that way."

"Can you milk?"

"Yes."

"The next question is, how much did you calculate to get?" asked Brackett, cautiously.

"Peter told me how much you gave him," said Andy.

Mr. Brackett was glad to hear this, as he

knew that most boys expected larger wages. He was glad that Andy knew what his predecessor had received.

"Yes," he said, with the air of a liberal man, "I gave Peter fifty cents a week, though he wasn't really worth it.   Fifty cents and board, and lodgings, and washing," he added, by way of making the salary seem as munificent as possible.

"It doesn't seem to me very high pay," said Andy, who thought it politic to drive a bargain.

"Remember, you're only a boy," said Mr. Brackett, "and boys can't do as much as men. Fifty cents is excellent pay for a boy of—how old be you?"

"Sixteen."

"For a boy of sixteen.   Of course, when you're a man grown, you can get a good deal more.   Why, I pay one man as much as a dollar and a quarter a day!"

"Would I have to work very hard?" asked Andy.

"Oh, no!   Just enough for healthy exercise," said Brackett, in a light, cheerful tone. "It does boys good to use their limbs.   I was a dreadful hard worker when I was a boy."

"You look as if you'd been tired ever since," said Andy to himself, as he watched the lounging attitude of his future employer.

"You'll have a nice, pleasant home," continued Mr. Brackett—"plenty of life and fun.

I've got four beautiful children, that'll look upon you as a brother. Mrs. Brackett, who is a perfect lady, will take an interest in you and make you feel at home."

Before Andy could reply, Mrs. Brackett made her appearance at the back door.

"Jeremiah!" she screamed. "I want some more wood—quick!"

"All right, Lucindy. Well, what do you say? Will you come?"

"I'll try it a week," said Andy.

"Then you can begin by sawing and splitting some wood. There's the wood pile, and there's the saw and ax. You'd better work up at a pretty good quantity."

"Well, I've got rid of that job," thought Brackett, with a sigh of relief. "He looks like a good, strong boy. I hope I'll be able to keep him."

CHAPTER XXXII.

TOMMY'S INNOCENT TRICK.

It was not till supper-time that Andy was introduced to the members of Mr. Brackett's family.

"I hope you'll do better than the last boy," said Mrs Brackett.

"I hope so," said Andy.

Here Mr. Dodge entered the room.

"Father, I've hired a new boy," said Mr. Brackett.

" I see you have," replied the old man, demurely, looking at Andy as if he had never
seen him before. " What's his name? "

" Henry Miller."

" I am glad to see you, Henry," said the old
gentleman, with a smile.

" Thank you, sir ! "

Just then Andy felt his next neighbor at
the table, Tommy, trying to stick a pin into
his leg. It was one of the engaging tricks of
Mr. Brackett's promising heir.

Now, Andy was not inclined to submit to
anything of the kind, and he forcibly took the
pin from the hands of the young mischief-
maker.

" Gimme my pin! " screamed Tommy.

For answer, Andy stuck it into his coat
lapel on the opposite side.

" Have you got Tommy's pin? " asked Mrs.
Brackett, angrily.

" Yes, ma'am," answered Andy.

" Give it right back to him ! "

" So I will, after supper; but I object to his
using my leg for a pincushion," answered our
hero, coolly.

Mrs. Brackett's temper was not of the best.

" Do you hear that, Mr. Brackett? " she
snapped.

" Hear what, Lucinda? "

" Hear that boy defy me to my face? "

" I guess you'd better give Tommy his pin,"

said Mr. Brackett, who stood in awe of his wife.

"You must excuse me, sir, unless you give him a different place at the table," said Andy, firmly, but with perfect politeness.

"Come here and sit by your mother, my angel!" said Mrs. Brackett.

As Tommy rose to obey, Andy, with a smile, restored to him his pin.

I am sorry to relate the sequel. Tommy, emboldened by his success, seized an opportunity playfully to prick his mother, and found that he had made a decided blunder. The lady instantly seized the young culprit by the collar and dragged him from the room, shaking him vigorously.

"I'll learn you to play tricks on your ma!" she exclaimed, angrily. "Not another mouthful shall you have to eat to-night, you saucy little imp! But what can be expected when your father upholds you in your bad actions?"

"Really, Lucindy," exclaimed Mr. Brackett, justly astonished, "I don't understand you!"

Mrs. Brackett volunteered no explanation, but flounced back to her seat, and the remainder of the meal was passed in solemn and dreary silence.

Andy was very much amused at the sudden change in Mrs. Brackett's sentiments toward her angel boy, but of course said nothing.

Later in the evening he got a chance to

speak a few words, unobserved, with the old gentleman.

"You did right, Henry," said Mr. Dodge— '(It was decided from motives of prudence that he had better call our hero by this name)— "in showing that young torment that he couldn't play tricks on you. He is about the worst behaved boy I know."

"Does he ever trouble you, sir?"

"No; not much. His parents think it would not be politic to let him."

"Mrs. Brackett seems a very agreeable woman," said Andy, laughing.

"She's a good deal worse than her husband. She is very bad-tempered, mean and disagreeable. She isn't lazy, like her husband, but he is better natured than she. How do you think you shall like staying here?"

"I wouldn't stay a day longer if it were not for you, sir."

"Thank you, Henry! You are a good boy. I shan't stay long myself, but there are some things I must attend to before I can go away."

Here Brackett came in sight, and the two separated, not wishing to excite his suspicions.

CHAPTER XXXIII.

MR. DODGE'S MYSTERIOUS JOURNEY.

ANDY soon found that his position was by no means an easy one. Though Mr. Brackett was a lazy man himself, he had no notion of allowing his hired boy to imitate his example. Even if he had been inclined to be indulgent, Mrs. Brackett would have taken care that Andy had enough to do. She had taken a dislike to our hero, dating from the first supper when Andy firmly resisted little Tommy's attempt to use him as a cushion.

"I don't know what you think, Mr. Brackett," said his wife, one day, about a week after Andy's term of service began, but I consider that new boy of yours an impudent, good-for-nothing upstart!"

"He is a good worker, Lucindy," said Mr. Brackett. "He does more work than any boy I ever had."

"Maybe he does and maybe he doesn't, but that ain't the point."

"It is the point with me, my dear. Between ourselves, we get him very cheap. I don't believe I could get another boy that would do so much work for fifty cents a week."

"Fifty cents a week seems to me very good wages," answered Mrs. Brackett, whose ideas of compensation were not very liberal.

"I think it's enough myself for an ordinary boy; but Henry is uncommonly smart."

"He feels uncommonly smart, I can tell you that," retorted the lady. "Why, Brackett, he seems to consider himself of as much importance as you or I."

This was quite true. Andy had gauged Mr. and Mrs. Brackett pretty accurately, and felt a decided contempt for them both. Both were mean, one lazy and the other ill-tempered, while neither was up to the average in refinement or education. So he was disposed to rate himself considerably higher than either; and who of my young readers will deny that he has a right to do so?

"Well, Lucindy," continued Brackett, in a pacific tone, "it doesn't make any difference to us what the boy thinks of himself. If he chooses to make himself ridiculous by his airs, why let him, for all I care."

"But there's something more, Mr. Brackett," said his wife.

"What more?"

"The way he treats Tommy. You haven't forgotten how he treated him at supper the very first night?"

"Tommy was trying to prick him with a pin. You couldn't expect him to stand that?"

"He could have mentioned it to you or me, then. Instead of that, what does he do? Why, he seizes the poor child's hand and pulls the pin away from him. You ought to have flogged him for it."

"You didn't seem to like it yourself when Tommy attacked you with a pin," said Mr. Brackett, laughing. "You didn't stand on any ceremony, but hauled the boy out of the room," and Mr. Brackett unguardedly laughed at the recollection.

His wife reddened and inquired, sharply:

" So you choose to compare me to your hired boy, do you, Mr. Brackett?"

" Not that I know of, Lucindy."

" You seem to think it makes no difference whether Tommy pricks him or me—his ma and your wife," said Mrs. Brackett, severely.

" Really, Lucindy, you twist my words so I don't know hardly what I do mean."

" I want you to stand by your own flesh and blood, Mr. Brackett. I don't want you to allow them to be imposed on and ill-treated by a young tramp whom you have hired to do chores."

" I don't mean to. What do you expect me to do, anyway?"

" I expect you to teach that boy his place."

" If I don't treat him well he won't stay. He'll leave me all of a sudden, as Peter did."

" Then you can get another boy."

" That isn't so easily done as you may suppose. I can't get any of the boys round here to work for me—I'm sure I don't know why— and new ones don't come along every day. I don't fancy being left without one to do the chores myself."

" If you did them all, you wouldn't work as hard as I do," said his wife, contemptuously, and not altogether without a basis of truth.

" You can't expect a woman to know anything about a man's work," said Mr. Brackett, in a complacent tone of superiority.

"I know I could do all your work, and get done in half the day," said his wife.

Mr. Brackett shrugged his shoulders, and was about to saunter off, when his father-in-law made his appearance.

"Mr. Brackett," said he, "if you can spare Henry and your horse and team, I would like to have him drive me over to Jefferson this afternoon."

"Really, father," said Brackett, who did not like the proposal, for it would throw upon his shoulders some of Andy's work, "I'd like to oblige you, but it would be very inconvenient. You see, Henry's got his work to do, and——"

"I didn't ask it as a favor," said Mr. Dodge. "I mean to pay you for the boy's services, and also for the horse and team."

Now, money was the god of both Mr. and Mrs. Brackett, and this put quite a different face on the matter.

"Let father have the boy and team," said Mrs. Brackett. "You can spare them."

"It would be worth as much as two dollars," said Brackett.

"I will pay you two dollars," said Simon Dodge promptly.

Here a new and brilliant idea struck Mr. Brackett, and he said, briskly:

"I'll tell you what, father; I'll drive you over myself, instead of Henry, and I won't charge you a cent more, even if my time is more valuable than his."

He reflected that it would be easier driving round the country than staying at home and doing the boy's work.

"Thank you for your kind offer," said the old man, quietly, "but I can't accept it."

"You mean you'd rather have the boy drive you?" asked Mr. Brackett, in amazement.

"I would," answered his father-in-law, candidly.

"Really that doesn't seem friendly," said Mr. Brackett.

"I generally like to have my own way, Jeremiah," said Mr. Dodge, quietly. "I don't mind allowing you two dollars and a half, which is more than I should need to pay at the stable. Is it yes or no?"

"Oh, of course, I agree," said Brackett, rather disappointed. "Do you want to go now?"

"Yes."

"What in the world is he going to do?" thought Mr. and Mrs. Brackett; for this was a request out of the ordinary course. "It must be something he doesn't want us to know."

Doubtful as to how much information they could extract from Andy, a sharp plan suggested itself to Mrs. Brackett.

"Father," said she, "have you any objection to taking Tommy along with you? The dear boy loves to be with his grandpa, and he can sit between you and Henry. He doesn't take up much room."

" I won't take him this afternoon, Lucinda,"
said Mr. Dodge, mildly.

" The poor child would enjoy it so much to
ride with his grandpa," pleaded Mrs. Brackett.

" Tommy must wait till another time," said
" grandpa," firmly.

Mrs. Brackett was displeased, and, though
she did not venture to say anything more, she
showed by her manner that she considered her
poor boy was slighted.

The team was soon ready, and the old man
rode off with our hero.

Mr. and Mrs. Brackett looked after them,
with a look of baffled curiosity.

" What does this mean, Jeremiah?" asked
his wife, at last.

" That's more than I can tell, Lucindy," returned her husband.

" Seems mighty mysterious to me."

" So it does."

" If he'd only have taken Tommy, the dear
child would have told us just where he went
and what he did."

" So he would. Maybe that was what he was
afraid of."

" I've been thinkin'——"

" Well, what have you been thinkin', Jeremiah?" asked his wife, impatient at her husband's pause.

" I've been thinkin' that perhaps father is
going to make his will this afternoon."

" Why shouldn't he let us know?"

"Oh, perhaps he wants to surprise us."

"Jeremiah, do you think there is any fear of his leaving his property to them relations of his in the East?"

"I can't say, but I guess not. He never hears from them. Like as not, he doesn't know where they live."

"We must find out, some way, whether he makes a will, and what's in it," said Mrs. Brackett, nodding vigorously. "When they get home, try to get it out of the boy what the old man did, and where he went."

"I will, Lucindy."

CHAPTER XXXIV.

WHAT MR. DODGE DID IN JEFFERSON.

ANDY had no previous intimation that he would be called upon to drive Mr. Dodge over to Jefferson, but he was very glad to do so.

When they were fairly started, Mr. Dodge said:

"Henry, probably Mr. and Mrs. Brackett will cross-examine you on our return, to learn where I went and what I did. They are very curious on that subject—so much so that Mr. Brackett offered to drive me over himself."

"I won't tell them," said Andy, very promptly.

"You might find it a little awkward to refuse," said the old man, "and for this reason I will not tell you precisely."

"That will be the best way," answered Andy, who was not troubled by idle curiosity.

"I will only say that the business I have to do will help prepare the way for our departure."

"I am glad of that, sir, for I don't much enjoy being in Mr. Brackett's employment."

"It will soon be over, Henry, and I will take care that you lose nothing by what you are doing in my behalf."

"I don't want to be paid for that, Uncle Simon."

"Have you heard from your mother since you came here?"

"No, sir; I have not dared to write, for fear the letter might be seen by Mr. Brackett or his wife."

"You shall have an opportunity of writing from Jefferson. We will drive directly to the hotel and put up our team. You can write your letter in the hotel while I am out attending to my business."

Andy was very glad of this permission, for he knew that his mother would feel anxious till she had heard of his safe arrival.

When the team was disposed of, Andy entered the hotel office.

Jefferson was the shire town of the county, and was therefore at times the resort of a considerable number of visitors. For this reason it required and possessed a very commodious hotel.

At the desk Andy saw a pleasant-looking boy of about his own age, whose name, as he afterward learned, was George Tierney. The boy looked social and friendly, and he addressed him.

" Can you let me have a sheet of paper and an envelope? " he asked.

" Certainly," said George, briskly. " Do you want to write a letter? "

" Yes, I should like to do so."

" You will find a table and ink in there," said George, pointing to a small room leading from the office. " Of course you will want a postage stamp."

" Yes, I would like one."

George produced one, and Andy paid for it. Then our hero, who had thought of a plan for carrying on a correspondence with his mother, asked:

" Would you be willing to do me a favor? "

" Of course I would," said George, pleasantly—" that is, unless you want to borrow a thousand dollars," he added, with a laugh. " I could not oblige you there."

" It isn't anything of that kind. I want to know if I may have a letter directed to me in your care? "

" Of course; but why don't you have it sent to where you live? "

" There is an objection which I can't mention just now."

" Where do you live? "

"Over at Cato. I am working for Mr. Brackett, a farmer."

George whistled.

"I thought so when I saw you with Mr. Dodge," he said. "I worked there once myself."

"You did? How long did you stay?" inquired Andy, with interest.

"I stood it a week," laughed George, "and then left. I came here, where I have an excellent place. Mr. Jones, the landlord, treats me tiptop."

"I should think you'd like it a good deal better."

"Can't you get a better place?" asked George, in a tone of sympathy.

"I am willing to stay for the present," said Andy. "Mr. Dodge is kind to me."

"Yes, he is a kind man. "If Brackett had been as good, I would have stayed longer, though I only got fifty cents a week. Did you ever hear of such mean pay?"

"That's what I get myself," answered Andy.

"You won't get rich on it very soon."

"No, I don't expect to."

Andy went into the adjoining room and wrote his letter. He had finished it, and given it to George Tierney to mail, when Mr. Dodge returned.

Though the old gentleman did not mention the nature of the business in which he had been engaged, we may state that he had been to the office of the lawyer with whom he had for years been on friendly and confidential terms, and there executed a will, which gave his entire property, invested in stocks and bonds, to his niece, Mrs. Gordon, in trust for Andy, to become the property of our hero when he should have attained his majority. He named the lawyer as his executor.

"There," he said, when the document was duly signed and attested, "that takes a burden from my mind."

"What would the Bracketts say if they knew what you have done this day?" said the lawyer, smiling; for between him and his client there were no secrets.

"They have no right to feel disappointed," said the old man, "for I have acted very generously by them. I gave them half of all I had, and I didn't wait till my death to do it."

"You have dealt a good deal more generously by them than I would have done," said the lawyer, emphatically.

"If it were to do over again, I would act differently; but what is done can't be undone. Perhaps it is all for the best."

On the way home Mr. Dodge seemed to be in unusually good spirits. As he had said to the lawyer, he felt that a burden had been lifted from his mind. He had made his will and provided that his property should go where he wished it to go, and felt no further anxiety on that point.

But if he felt no anxiety, Mr. and Mrs. Brackett did.

They felt that something was in the wind. Mr. Dodge must have some object in going to Jefferson and refusing the company of his son-in-law, and even of dear Tommy.

They waited impatiently for the return of the team, and were on the alert when it drove into the yard.

"Did you have a pleasant ride, father?" asked Brackett.

"Yes, Jeremiah, thank you."

"Did you attend to all your business, or will you want the horse another day?"

"I didn't say I went on business," said the old man, shrewdly. "I may want the horse another day. Here is your money, Jeremiah."

Mr. Brackett extended his hand with alacrity, and took the proffered two dollars and a half, which he put in his pocket.

"You can have it any time, father," he said. "I'm always ready to oblige you."

Mr. Dodge went into the house, leaving Andy in the hands of his son-in-law.

"Did father call round much over in Jefferson, Henry?" asked Mr. Brackett, with an assumption of careless indifference.

"No, sir," answered Andy, demurely.

"Where did he go?" pursued Brackett, in

the same tone, but with an expression of restrained eagerness.

"He drove right to the hotel," answered Andy.

"Yes, but after that?"

"He put up the horse there, and left me there."

"He did!" ejaculated Brackett, disappointed.

"Yes."

"Did he leave the hotel?"

"Yes, but he didn't tell me where he went."

Brackett looked hard at Andy, to see if he were keeping anything back, but our hero's manner was perfectly honest and sincere, and he was forced to conclude that the boy knew nothing more than himself of Mr. Dodge's errand.

"I didn't think father was so sharp," said Brackett to his wife. "He wouldn't let the boy know where he went."

But Mr. Brackett had his curiosity satisfied, after all. One of his neighbors had been over to Jefferson the same afternoon, and reported to the farmer that he had seen Mr. Dodge coming out of the office of Mr. Brief, the lawyer.

"What was he doing there?" thought Brackett, perplexed. "Did he make a will? That's what I would like to know."

But that was a question more easily asked than answered.

CHAPTER XXXV.

TOMMY'S PRANKS.

TOMMY BRACKETT may have been an angel in the eyes of an indulgent mother, but most people who had anything to do with him regarded him as a perverse and mischievous imp. He had always been a thorn in the side of the successive boys who had been employed by Mr. Brackett. The little boy was quite aware of his position as the son of the master of the house, and felt at liberty to tease and annoy his father's hired boys in any manner that presented itself to his ingenious fancy.

As we already know, he had made a beginning with Andy at the very first meal of which the latter partook of at the farm, but somehow the experiment did not succeed. Instead of submitting, our hero had very coolly and composedly deprived him of the pin, which he had selected as a means of annoyance.

Tommy was rather surprised, but he was not disposed to give up at the failure of the first attempt. He was encouraged, indeed, by his mother taking his part against Andy, though she resented any trick upon herself.

Andy was naturally fond of children. Had Tommy been a well-behaved boy, he would have regarded him with favor and affection, but he very soon decided that any such feeling for his employer's son was not deserved and would be thrown away.

One morning, as Tommy was wondering what he should do for amusement, his attention was drawn to the family cat, which was dozing in the yard, unconscious of danger.

" I'll have some fun with you, puss," said he. " Come along! "

He took the cat and drew her to the trough at which the cattle were accustomed to drink. Seizing the poor animal by the head, he thrust it into the water till the poor thing was near strangulation. Of course, she made her dissatisfaction known by shrill cries.

They attracted the attention of Andy, who was splitting wood only a few rods distant. Looking up, he saw the poor cat's predicament, and became justly indignant.

" What are you doing there, Tommy? " he demanded, sternly.

Tommy looked up and answered with characteristic impudence:

" None of your business! "

" Stop hurting the cat! " said Andy, imperatively.

" Go on with your work and let me alone," answered Tommy, preparing to plunge the cat's head into the trough once more.

Andy's answer was to drop the ax and rush to the trough. Seizing the boy by the collar, he forcibly took away the cat and said:

" You ought to be ashamed of your cruelty! "

How dare you touch me? " demanded Tommy, furiously, stamping his foot.

"It doesn't require much daring, you mischievous little scamp!" said Andy.

"I'll get my father to turn you away," threatened Tommy.

"Just as you like," said Andy, amused. "I am doing him a favor by staying; and he knows it."

"I'll get him to give you a flogging!" said Tommy, finding that the first threat had very little effect.

"If he would give you a sound whipping, it's only what you deserve," said our hero, going back to his work.

"He wouldn't whip me. My mother wouldn't let him!" said Tommy.

Andy laughed. He was disposed to think that the boy was only telling the truth, since Mrs. Brackett appeared to have her husband under her thumb, as he had already found out.

Tommy felt outraged by the thought that his father's hired boy had dared to lay hands on him, and thirsted for revenge. If he had only been stronger than Andy, our hero would have stood a chance of a thrashing then and there; but, unfortunately for Tommy, his strength was not equal to his spirit.

"What shall I do?" he thought.

He waited till he got a few rods away, and picking up a pebble, threw it at Andy. It whizzed within a foot of our hero's face.

Andy looked up, and saw the boy laughing with evident enjoyment.

"Did you fire that stone, Tommy?" he asked.

"Yes, I did."

"What did you do it for?"

"I'll do it again!"

And Tommy suited the action to the word.

Andy was upon him in a moment, and seized him as he was entering the back door.

"Ma!" yelled Tommy, at the top of his voice. "Come here! Henry's murdering me!"

Mrs. Brackett rushed to the door, her hands covered with dough, and her indignation was intense when she saw her darling in the grasp of her husband's hired boy.

"What's all this?" she exclaimed. "Let go my child, you young ruffian! How dare you?"

"Mrs. Brackett," said Andy, "Tommy has been firing stones at me. If you will make him stop, I shall let him alone."

"You have no business to touch him, anyway! I'll make you smart for it!" exclaimed the angry woman. "I presume you are telling lies about my poor child. Tell me all about it, Tommy. Did you fire a stone at him?"

"Yes; but he began it."

"How did he begin it?"

"He took the cat away from me," exclaimed the virtuous Tommy.

"Did you take the cat away from my boy?" demanded Mrs. Brackett, in a tragical tone

"Yes, ma'am."

" How dared you do it? "

" Because he was teasing it. If I had not interfered, he would have drowned her. He was putting her head into the trough."

" 'Tain't so, ma! Don't you believe him! " vociferated Tommy, with unblushing falsehood.

" I don't believe it," said Mrs. Brackett, forcibly. " I know he is telling lies about you, my angel! "

Andy was not in the least excited, but he was rather amused.

" You may believe it or not, Mrs. Brackett," he said. " I only tell you that it is so."

" Tain't so! 'tain't so! " yelled Tommy.

" Of course it isn't," said his mother. " I won't believe any of that bad boy's lies. Go back to your work, you young brute; and take care how you touch my darling boy again."

" You had better advise him not to touch me again, Mrs. Brackett," said Andy.

And, without waiting for an answer, he went back to his work.

Not a word was said to Tommy about what he had done, and he was emboldened to continue his persecutions.

Five minutes afterward, he went out into the yard again and shied a stone at Andy's head.

Our hero was prepared. He sprang for Tommy, seized him, and drawing him to the trough, took a dipper of water, and dashed it into his face.

"The next time you'll get something worse," he said, coolly.

Tommy roared with anger and mortification, and again ran into the house, to complain to his mother.

She came out like an avenging fury, and began to revile Andy, and threaten all sorts of punishment when her husband got home.

"Do you expect me to stand still, and let Tommy throw stones at me?" asked Andy.

"I didn't throw a stone," denied Tommy.

"Of course you didn't, my angel!" said Mrs. Brackett. "Henry Miller, when Mr. Brackett gets home, he shall whip you till you are black and blue."

"Mrs. Brackett," said an indignant voice behind her, "you are blaming the wrong boy. Tommy did throw stones at Henry, for I saw the whole transaction from my window. Henry treated him just as he ought to be treated. If he were my boy, I would give him a good, sound whipping."

Knowing that Mr. Dodge had money to leave, Mrs. Brackett did not dare to reply as she wished to do.

"So you turn against my poor boy, too," she said.

"I tell the truth about him," said the old man, disgusted. "Had he treated me as he has Henry, I would make him suffer."

Mrs. Brackett was white with anger, but she did not dare to show it.

"Come into the house, Tommy," she said. "It seems you have no friends but your mother. Even your grandpa turns against you."

"I thank Heaven he is not my grandson!" said Mr. Dodge, after mother and child had left the the scene. "Henry, don't let that little rascal impose upon you, or his mother either."

"I won't, sir," assured Andy, firmly.

From that moment Mrs. Brackett positively hated Andy, and anxiously sought for some means of revenge.

CHAPTER XXXVI.

MR. BRACKETT'S DIPLOMACY.

MRS. BRACKETT took the earliest opportunity of informing her husband of the way in which Andy had abused poor Tommy, but he did not enter wholly into her feeling of resentment, not being quite so blind to the faults of his oldest cherub as Tommy's mother.

He was still more disinclined to move in the matter when he learned that his father-in-law had taken Andy's part.

"We've got to move slow, wife," he said, cautiously. "We don't want to stir up the old man."

"Father ought to be ashamed to turn

against his own grandson," said Mrs. Brackett, indignantly.

"If we come to that, Tommy isn't exactly Mr. Dodge's grandson."

"Well, it's the same thing," persisted his wife. "He seems to think more of this new boy than of poor Tommy."

"It won't do to make a fuss about it, Lucindy. We must be patient, and humor the old man. He's seventy-five years old, and can't live much longer."

"That's what you've been saying for the last five years," grumbled Mrs. Brackett. "I don't see, for my part, but he's likely to live till you and I are in our graves."

"Not as bad as that, Lucindy. I'm getting a little anxious to have him make a will. I don't want him to die till he's left the property to us, safe and sure."

"It would go to us anyway, wouldn't it, Jeremiah?"

"It ought to, but there's those Eastern relations. They might claim it."

"That would be shameful!" said Mrs. Brackett, warmly.

"So it would—so it would, Lucindy. I'll tell you what, I'll speak to the old man about it this very day."

"I wish you would."

"So you see we'd better not irritate him by scolding Henry."

"I suppose you're right, Jeremiah," assented

Mrs. Brackett, reluctantly; "but I was in hopes you would give him a good flogging."

"It wouldn't be politic, Lucindy, just at this time."

"Is he going to abuse my poor darling without anybody's interfering?" demanded Mrs. Brackett, discontentedly.

"No. I'll speak to him about it."

Accordingly, Mr. Brackett sought out Andy, and said:

"Henry, I hear there was some trouble this morning between you and Tommy."

"Yes, sir. Did Mrs. Brackett tell you about it?"

"Yes. She is very angry."

"I think I have more reason to be angry, sir."

"She says you dragged him into the house by the collar, and afterward threw water in his face."

"Did she tell you what Tommy did to me?" asked Andy.

"She said he was rather playful, and that you got mad."

"He playfully fired stones at my head," said Andy. "If he had hit me I should have been severely hurt. I don't like that kind of playfulness."

"I know he is a mischievous boy. Still, you should remember that he is a little boy, much younger and smaller than you are."

"So I did, and for that reason I wouldn't

hurt him. I don't think," continued Andy, " I could make up my mind to hurt a little boy. But I can't let him fire stones at me."

" I guess there has been no harm done, but you must try not to provoke Mrs. Brackett. She can't see any fault in Tommy, though I am not so blind."

" I certainly shall let him alone if he will let me alone, and I won't hurt him, at any rate. I will only defend myself if he tries to play any tricks on me."

Mr. Brackett seemed to be satisfied, and Andy was disposed to think favorably of him, not being aware that he was moderate and reasonable because he did not think it politic to be otherwise.

Just at this moment Mr. Dodge came out of the house, and Mr. Brackett decided to attack him on the subject of the will.

" How do you feel, father? " he inquired.

" Very well, thank you, Jeremiah," said Mr. Dodge, rather surprised at his son-in-law's solicitude.

" You are remarkably well for a man of your age, as I was remarking to Lucindy yesterday. By the way, how old are you, father? "

" Seventy-five years last birthday," answered the old man, " but I don't feel any older than I did fifteen years ago."

" Just so! Still, you are older; but I suppose you've fixed things so you've no worldly anxieties? "

"I think I've got enough to carry me through, Jeremiah."

"Of course you have, father; and more, too. You can't begin to spend your income?"

This was said in an inquiring tone, but the old gentleman did not make any reply.

"It's only prudent to make your will, father, for, of course, a man of your age may be cut off sudden. Death comes like a thief in the night," added Mr. Brackett, utilizing one of the few passages of Scripture with which he happened to be acquainted.

"I dare say you are right, Jeremiah," said Mr. Dodge, with a smile.

"You mustn't think I am anxious on my own account," said Mr. Brackett. "Of course, money's a consideration to me, and I'm willing to have you fix things as you think best. But don't you think you would feel better if you had things all fixed straight and sure on paper?"

"Perhaps you are right, Mr. Brackett," said his father-in-law, with the same provoking smile, which Mr. Brackett was utterly unable to understand.

"I feel kinder delicate about speaking of it," pursued Mr. Brackett, "but I thought I ought to do it. Folks are so apt to put off the important duty to the last."

"By the way, Jeremiah, have you made your will?" asked the old man.

"I?" ejaculated Mr. Brackett, in surprise.

" Yes."

" No; I can't say I have."

" You'd better think of it. You're not as old as I am, but men younger than you die every day."

" You don't think I'm looking poorly, do you? " queried Mr. Brackett, nervously.

" Oh, no! And I hope I am not. Still, you may die before me."

" That's so, of course; but it ain't hardly likely."

" No; I hope you won't. I hope you will live to be as old as I am."

" I'll tell you what, father," said Brackett, cunningly, " I'll make my will if you make yours."

" I'll think of it, Jeremiah," said Mr. Dodge, politely.

" Confound the old man! I can't get anything out of him," said Brackett to himself. " I think he teases me on purpose. The idea of thinking he doesn't need to make a will because I don't! One thing's pretty certain, though—he hasn't made his will yet. If he should die without one, I will prevent them Eastern relations from hearing of it, if I can. I ought to have that property—and I mean to."

Mr. Dodge smiled to himself when his son-in-law left him.

" Mr. Brackett thinks he is shrewd," he said to himself, " but his shrewdness and cunning are of a very transparent character. What would he say if he knew that I have already made my will, and that his name is not mentioned in it? What would he say if he knew that my chief heir is at present in his employ, working for fifty cents a week? I suspect there would be a storm—in fact, a hurricane.

"Henry," said the old man, to our hero, "has Mr. Brackett spoken to you about your little trouble with Tommy?"

"Yes, sir."

"Was he angry?"

"No, he spoke very reasonably. I have no fault to find with what he said."

"He isn't quite such a fool as his wife, nor is he as ill-tempered. If I had given the Bracketts all my property, reserving none to myself, I should be in a bad position. Fortunately I was saved from such folly."

"It strikes me," reflected Mrs. Brackett, looking out of the kitchen window, "that father's pretty thick with that boy of ours. If I had my way, I'd send him packing. He's a low, artful boy, and if I were Mr. Brackett, I would send him off, if I had to do his work myself."

Jeremiah Brackett, however, was by no no means of his wife's opinion. He appreciated the fact that Henry Miller—to use the name by which he knew him—was more faithful and a more steady worker than any of his predecessors, and he did not mean to part with him for any light cause, his wife's prejudices to the contrary, notwithstanding.

Half an hour later, Andy was destined to a considerable surprise.

CHAPTER XXXVII.
AN OLD ACQUAINTANCE TURNS UP.

"Boy, does Mr. Brackett live here?"

Andy looked up from his work, and saw standing at a little distance a man, apparently about thirty years of age.

He started in amazement, for he had no difficulty in recognizing the younger of the two highwaymen who had so nearly robbed him of the money intrusted to him by the Misses Peabody. There are cases of remarkable resemblance, but Andy was a close observer, and he was satisfied this was not such a case, but that the companion of Mike Hogan stood before him.

Owing to his surprise, he delayed answering the question.

"Well, boy, what are you gaping at?" demaded the young man, impatiently. "Did you hear my question?"

"Excuse me, sir! Yes, Mr. Brackett does live here."

"Is Mrs. Brackett at home?" continued the newcomer.

"Yes, sir."

"Well, pilot me in, then," said the other, carelessly. "Are you Brackett's hired boy?"

"Yes, sir."

"Well, it seems to me he might get a smarter one."

"I was smart enough to foil you once, Mr. Highwayman," thought Andy; but he only answered, "Very likely he might."

"Come, that's candid! It makes me think better of you. Go ahead, and I'll follow."

"What does this robber want of Mrs. Brackett, I wonder?" thought Andy. "Ought I to warn her of his character?"

Mrs. Brackett was ironing in the kitchen, when Andy entered, followed by the stranger. She was not feeling very good-natured, and jumped to the conclusion that the intruder was a peddler.

"Henry," said she, sharply, "what makes you bring a peddler into the house? You know I never have anything to do with them."

Andy was going to plead in excuse that the stranger had inquired particularly for her, but he was spared the trouble.

"I must say, Lucinda," said the young man, bursting out laughing, "that you give a curious reception to your only brother."

"George, is it really you?" exclaimed Mrs. Brackett, laying down her flatiron, in surprise and joy.

"I reckon it is. How are you, old girl?"

Mrs. Brackett, who was really attached to her younger brother, advanced eagerly and imprinted a kiss on his cheek, and began to express her wonder at his sudden appearance.

Andy, concluding that his presence was no longer required, left the kitchen, and returned to work.

He, too, was full of surprise.

"It is strange enough that the man who tried to rob me should be the brother of my employer's wife," he soliloquized. "Of course, she can't be aware of his mode of life."

Was Andy called upon to inform her? He decided not, but if this man took up his residence for any length of time at Mr. Brackett's house, he would feel compelled to watch him narrowly, lest he should fall into his old dishonest practices.

"He didn't recognize me," Andy reflected, with satisfaction. "If he had, he might have tried to do me an injury lest I should betray him."

Meanwhile, the brother and sister were chatting together in the kitchen.

"What have you been doing, George?" asked Mrs. Brackett. "Why is it that you have been silent for so long?"

"Oh, I've been drifting about, Lucinda!" said her brother.

"But haven't you been engaged in any business?" asked his sister.

"Oh, well, part of the time I've been a collector," said George, with a quizzical smile.

He did not care to explain that his collecting had been from unoffending travelers, nor did he care to mention that he had served a three-years' term at Sing Sing prison, under an assumed name.

"It must be eight years since we met, George," went on Mrs. Brackett.

"Is it as long as that?" said George, indifferently.

"Yes, I know it is, for my dear little Tommy was a baby, and now he is a fine boy of eight years."

"Inherits your sweet disposition, Lucinda, I suppose," said her brother, banteringly.

"You always would have your joke, George," said Mrs. Brackett, coloring and looking annoyed.

"Have you got any more children, Lucinda?"

"Yes—three more."

"They must be a great nuisance," said her brother, shrugging his shoulders.

"You were a nuisance when you were a small boy," said his sister, with spirit.

"I dare say I was. Well, how are you and Brackett getting along?"

"We ain't getting rich," said Mrs. Brackett, with a critical glance at her brother, as if to determine whether he was likely to want assistance.

He seemed very well dressed, and she hoped his circumstances were good, for, though she was attached to him, she was, on the whole, more attached to her money.

"You seem to be pretty prosperous," said George.

"Oh, yes! We have enough to eat, and drink and wear, but we can't save any money."

Mrs. Brackett conveniently forgot the five hundred dollars which she had in the savings bank.

"Is the old man Dodge still living?"

"He's living, and likely to live," said his sister, in a dissatisfied tone.

"Must be most a hundred, isn't he?"

"He's seventy-five, and can eat as much as a young man."

"How about the property? Is it all fixed right?" asked her brother, now showing some genuine interest.

"He gave Jeremiah the farm some years ago, but he won't give anything else, and we have to give him his board out of it."

"Has he got much money besides?"

"He must have somewhere from ten to fifteen thousand dollars."

"Whew! that's a pile! It will go to you in the end, won't it?"

"I don't know; it ought to. But he's got some relations off in the East, who may come in."

"Then you must get him to make a will in your favor."

"I wish he would. Brackett's spoken to him about it more than once, but he can be very obstinate when he chooses."

"You must introduce me to the old chap. Perhaps I can soften his obstinacy. I'm rather soft-spoken when I choose to be."

"You'll stay and make us a visit, won't you, George?"

"Yes, I'll stay a few days. I am tired of work, and shall find it pleasant to rest a while. Where's Brackett?"

"Here he is."

Mr. Brackett entered the kitchen at this moment, and glanced with some surprise at the young man, whom he did not at first recognize.

"It's brother George, Jeremiah," said Mrs. Brackett. "I don't wonder you don't recognize him, it's so long since we've seen him."

"How are you, George?" said his brother-in-law. "Where did you drop from?"

"Oh, I fancied I'd like to see you and Lucinda again, so I took the cars, and here I am."

"Business good with you, George?"

"Rather slow! Still, I've managed to live. You seem pretty comfortable."

Mr. Brackett shook his head.

"Farming's hard work and poor pay," he said. "I can't get ahead at all."

"When the old man pops off, you'll be pretty comfortable—hey?"

"I hope so; but there is no knowing how he'll leave the property."

"Mr. Brackett," said his wife, when they were alone, "we'd better not say anything to George about that money we've got in the savings bank. He might want to borrow it, and he was always careless about money."

"You're quite right, Lucindy," said her husband, approvingly. "You've got a long head of your own. I shall be silent as the grave. We had too hard work in laying it up to run any risk with it."

At supper the newcomer, George White, was introduced to Mr. Dodge and to Andy.

For the first time he seemed to see something familiar in our hero's face.

"It seems to me I've seen you somewhere before," he said.

"Perhaps you have," said Andy, indif-
erently. " Where ? "

"I suppose I'm mistaken," said White, looking puzzled ; "but you look some like a boy
I met some distance from here."

Andy forced himself to seem uninterested,
and George White dropped the subject, concluding that he was mistaken.

CHAPTER XXXVIII.

A WICKED COMPACT.

MRS. BRACKETT knew very little of the way in
which her brother had passed the last eight
years. She knew nothing of his lawless life
and conviction of crime, and supposed that his
record was as creditable as the average. She
was, therefore, quite ready to give him a cordial
welcome, and to consult him upon family matters. Through her influence, also Mr. Brackett
received his brother-in-law with a friendly welcome, acknowledging his claims as a relative.

As for George White, his object in seeking
out his sister after so long an absence may be
easily told. In fact, it was twofold. He was
hard up, and hoped that he might borrow a
sum of money from Lucinda, and also was
glad to betake himself to a quiet place so far
from New York, being quite too well known to
the police authorities of the metropolitan dis-
trict.

He at was present a fugitive from justice,
having recently made an attempt to enter a

house in Brooklyn, and failed, through the wakefulness of a member of the household.

Mr. and Mrs. Brackett and George White sat in a conclave together one evening soon after his arrival. They were discussing the obstinacy of Simon Dodge in deferring to make a will in favor of his disinterested son-in-law.

" Can't you persuade him to do it, Mr. Brackett ?" asked White.

" I've tried my best, and failed," said Brackett. " You see the old man's dreadfully obstinate when he sets about it. It's my opinion he's afraid to make a will for fear it will hasten his death."

" Maybe it would, if he made a will in your favor," said White, with a knowing wink at his brother-in-law.

" George, I am shocked at you ! " said his sister. " You shouldn't say such things. Suppose father should hear you ? "

" It might make him nervous, I dare say," said White, coolly. " Seems to me you act like a couple of children, you two. If I were in your place I'd see that a proper will was made."

" How would you manage it ? " asked Brackett.

" How would I manage it ? It's the simplest thing in the world. Is the old man's signature hard to imitate ? "

" You don't mean——" ejaculated Brackett, looking about him nervously.

" Yes, I do."

" But it would be forgery, and that is a serious offense."

"Nothing venture, nothing have!" said White, boldly. "The property ought to come to you and my sister. You agree to that, don't you?"

"Of course it ought," said Mr. Brackett. "Haven't we done everything for father, and slaved for his comfort?"

"Just so! And you ought to be rewarded. It's a very simple thing, as I have already said," continued White, shaking the ashes from his pipe.

Mr. Brackett was a little startled, but was not shocked. His morality was not of a high order, and he shrank from forgery only because it was a penal offense. He felt a little curious to inquire into the details of his brother-in-law's plan.

"Supposing I agreed to it," he said, cautiously, "I haven't any skill in imitating writing. I couldn't write a will that would look like father's."

"Only the signature would need to resemble his handwriting," said White. "I'm pretty good at imitating signatures myself," he added, carelessly. "Have you got any of the old man's writing?"

"Yes; I've got a letter here," said Brackett, going to his desk and producing one from a drawer.

"That could be imitated easily," said White, after a casual examination.

"I'll leave you two to talk business at your leisure," said Mrs. Brackett. "I must go upstairs and look after the children."

Her brother looked after her with a mocking smile.

"Lucinda's sharp and cautious," he remarked. "She thinks it best not to know anything about it, though she'll be ready enough to profit by it. Come, now, Brackett, I've a proposal to make."

"What is it?"

"I'll draw up such a will as you think best, and sign and witness it."

"That's very kind of you, George——"

"Hold on a minute! You don't suppose I'm so benevolent as to do all this without pay, do you?"

"I didn't know," answered Brackett, his jaw dropping.

"I'm not such an idiot, thank you! I must have a hundred dollars down, and a thousand dollars when you come into the property."

"That's rather steep!" said Brackett, disturbed.

"It isn't enough; but you are my sister's husband, and I'll work for you cheaper than for anyone else. I'd charge anybody else at least twice as much. Well, Brackett, what do you say?"

"It seems a great deal of money to pay for an hour's work. It won't take you more than an hour."

"You seem to forget there's some risk about it. Such work as that you can't measure by the time it takes."

"Lucindy would never agree to such terms as that."

"The more fool she! Didn't you tell me the old man was good for over ten thousand dollars?"

"Yes; he must have at least as much as that."

"And I ask only a thousand dollars to give it to you."

"Father might make a will himself, leaving it to us," suggested Brackett. "In that case, the money would be thrown away."

"You oughtn't to begrudge it to your wife's brother, even then," said White. "Still, I'll tell you what I'll do. If you get the money by any other will, you needn't pay me the thousand dollars. Isn't that fair?"

This proposal struck Mr. Brackett favorably, and this was the compact ultimately formed.

Mrs. Brackett opposed it strenuously at first, being unwilling to relinquish so much money, even in favor of her own brother; but she was at last persuaded that it would be better to have nine-tenths of the property than none at all, and consented.

Several conferences were held, and the date of the forged will was carefully discussed. At length it was decided to fix upon a time six months earlier, and to affix the names, as witnesses, of two men who then lived in the village, but had now gone West, and were not likely to return. Indeed, it was reported that one of them was dead, which, of course, would make it impossible for him to deny his signature.

One evening it chanced that Andy, who had

gone to the village, returned sooner than he intended on account of a sudden headache. In passing the window of the room where the conspirators were seated, he heard a chance word which arrested his attention.

The window, without the knowledge of Mr. and Mrs. Brackett, was slightly open, but this was hidden from view by the curtain, and through the aperture our hero had no difficulty in overhearing enough to satisfy him what was going on.

Of course his duty was clear. He must inform Mr. Dodge. The next morning an opportunity came. He not only told uncle Simon what his son-in-law was doing, but for the first time made him acquainted with the real character of Mrs. Brackett's brother.

Simon Dodge was silent for a time from amazement.

"I didn't think it possible," he said, "that Jeremiah Brackett would stoop to such a crime."

"I believe it is Mr. White who has put him up to it," said Andy.

"Perhaps you are right. At any rate, this confirms me in my resolution to go away. Next week, Henry, we will leave the old farm, where I have spent so many years, and in your mother's house I will spend the short time that remains to me."

"I am glad to hear you say so, Uncle Simon. I shall be very glad to get away myself."

"It is no longer safe for me to stay here," said the old man. "Once this will is forged, they will be impatient for me to die. As for their wicked scheming, it will avail them nothing. My true will is made, and in the hands of my lawyer, and is later than the date they have selected for the pretended one."

It was well that Mr. Dodge could not foresee the trying experience that awaited him before he could sunder the bonds that bound him to the old farm.

CHAPTER XXXIX.

A CUNNING PLOT.

GEORGE WHITE was a skillful penman—at one time he had been a bookkeeper—and he had no difficulty in drafting a will which might easily have passed for the genuine last will and testament of Simon Dodge.

It was shown to Mr. and Mrs. Brackett, and both were well satisfied with it.

"I guess this will make you all right, Jeremiah," said White. "It'll be worth a good deal of money to you."

"You're a master hand at the pen, George," said Brackett, admiringly. "Nobody will know this from the old man's signature. I'll take care of it till the time comes when it's wanted."

He held out his hand for the document, but George White drew back, smiling significantly.

"Not so fast, brother-in-law," he said. "You shall have this when I receive the hundred dollars. That was the bargain, you remember."

"You don't expect I've got a hundred dollars in cash, do you?" asked Brackett, disturbed.

"Then why did you agree to pay me that sum when I had done my work?" demanded White.

"I didn't think you'd insist on it. I'll tell you what I'll do. I'll give you a hundred and fifty when the money comes in to me."

"I am to have a thousand dollars then."

"Of course; and this will make eleven hundred and fifty. Come, that's a fair offer."

"It may be, in your eyes, brother-in-law, but it isn't in mine. I tell you I must have the money now."

"Where do you think I can raise so much money?" asked Brackett, who underrated White's penetration, or he would never have hoped to deceive him.

"Plenty of ways," replied White, coolly. "Your credit ought to be good for a loan of that amount, when you own a ten-thousand-dollar farm."

"There isn't anybody in town who has money to lend."

"Must be a peculiar place, then. Is there a mortgage on the farm?"

"No."

"Mortgage it, then, for a thousand dollars, pay me a hundred, and invest the rest."

"I don't believe Lucindy would agree to that."

"I see that I shall have to tear the will up."

"No, no; don't do that," said Brackett, hurriedly, extending his hand in alarm.

" I'll wait till to-morrow, then, and you can think over the matter. Talk with Lucinda, if you like. If she's wise, she'll agree to my demands."

Later in the day, George White found himself alone in the house. Mr. and Mrs. Brackett had gone to the village, taking the children with them.

" I think I'll make a voyage of discovery," said White. " I'll see if Lucinda hasn't got some money stowed away somewhere. It's a great wonder if she hasn't, for she's of a very mean and saving disposition, and, judging from the table she keeps, she doesn't spend all her income in pampering the appetites of her household."

He went upstairs stealthily, and opened the door of his sister's chamber. It was furnished like most bedrooms. Between the two windows stood the bureau, and to this George White instinctively made his way.

" Women always keep their valuables in their bureaus," said White.

And his experience as a burglar qualified him to express an opinion on this subject.

Generally Mrs. Brackett kept the drawers of her bureau locked, but to-day, by some oversight, she had left a key in one of the locks.

This easily enabled White to search them.

In a corner of the upper drawer his quick eye lighted on a savings-bank book, and he opened it eagerly.

" Five hundred dollars! " he exclaimed, triumphantly. " So it seems my poverty-stricken brother-in-law is not so poor, after all. He won't need to mortgage his farm to pay me my price. He and Lucinda were very cunning in keeping from me the knowledge of their savings, but it won't work—no, it won't work ! He must draw the money out of the bank for me to-morrow, or I destroy the will."

Just then a new thought occurred to White. Why couldn't he take the book, forge an order, and draw out the whole sum from the savings bank himself ? It tempted him, but prudence restrained him. It would be decidedly dangerous.

His sister and her husband were doubtless known in the next village, where the bank was located, and a stranger attempting to draw out money on their account would doubtless be subjected to suspicion, and probably be unable to accomplish his object.

" No, it won't do," White decided. " But I'll suggest to Brackett where he can find the money to pay me."

George White left his sister's room, and a sudden impulse led him to continue his investigations.

It has already been said that he had been struck by Andy's resemblance to some face he had seen before. It occurred to him after a while that the boy he resembled was the one who had baffled him in his attempt at robbery, on the highway, between Hamilton and Cranston.

But these towns were three hundred miles away, and it seemed far from likely that his brother-in-law's hired boy had been in that distant locality so recently. Moreover, Andy had not appeared to recognize him—though, as we know, he had done so.

White had asked him questions, nevertheless, designed to draw out information on this point, but Andy had skillfully evaded them, without exciting his suspicions.

Still, White was desirous of learning something more about Andy, and it was with this object in view that he went up the attic stairs and entered the little room occupied by our hero.

Andy had no trunk, but there was an old dressing table in the room, containing a shallow drawer.

White opened this drawer, and curiously scanned the contents.

Andy had incautiously left in the drawer a letter received from his mother, addressed to the care of his friend George Tierney, and it was of course postmarked Hamilton.

"Hamilton!" exclaimed White, in astonishment. "Henry receives letters from Hamilton! Why, that is the place where the boy lived who balked me, and had poor Mike Hogan arrested. It's the same boy, I'll bet fifty dollars! I saw the resemblance at once."

White opened the letter and read it through, and when he had finished, the whole secret was revealed to him.

He discovered that Andy was masquerading under an assumed name, that he was one of Simon Dodge's Eastern relatives, who, doubtless, were in opposition to the interests of his sister and her husband.

"Well, here's a conspiracy!" ejaculated White. "My sister has been cherishing a viper in her household, who is scheming to get possession of the old man's property. Was there ever anything more vile and treacherous?"

And the professional burglar became virtuously indignant.

Then an expression of triumph lighted up his face.

"I've found you out, my boy, and I'll put a spoke in your wheel," he said to himself. "I've got a little score of my own to settle with you, my young friend, and don't you forget it. Henry Miller, alias Andy Gordon, you'll find that you are no match for George White. Now, how shall I revenge myself on him?"

A bright idea occurred to White.

He went back to his sister's bedroom, took the savings-bank book, and carrying it up to the little attic chamber, put it in Andy's drawer, but away back in one corner, where the boy himself would not be likely to see it.

"There'll be lively times soon, I reckon," he said to himself, complacently.

CHAPTER XL.

THE BRACKETTS ARE CHECKMATED.

MR. AND MRS. BRACKETT got home about four o'clock. They had been talking over the proposal to pay White a hundred dollars cash,

but had not been able to make up their minds
to do it.

In fact, paying out ready money seemed as
bad to Mrs. Brackett—whose mean, parsimoni-
ous disposition has already been referred to—
as having a tooth drawn.

Indeed, I may say, confidentially, that she
would have preferred to lose half a dozen
teeth rather than part with a hundred dollars.

" We'll put George off," she said to her husband, as they were riding home.   " We'll pre-
tend that we are trying to raise the money, but
can't do it.   Perhaps he will get impatient and
agree to take less.   A hundred dollars is an
outrageous price for such a small job."

" So I think, Lucindy," chimed in her husband.   " Really your brother seems to me very
grasping."

" So he is, and very extravagant besides.
He could squander more money in a week than
we could lay by in six months."

Of course they would not have dared to dis-
cuss the subject in presence of the children ;
but they had been left behind, with the excep-
tion of the youngest, two years of age, to spend
the afternoon with some juvenile companions.

"It's lucky George doesn't know about our
account in the savings bank, Lucindy."

"If he knew of that, it would be impossible
to get rid of paying the money."

"Suppose he won't give up the will without
the whole amount down ?"

" He will.   It will do him no good, and if he
keeps it or destroys it he won't get a cent.   I

know he needs money, for he told me the other day that he was reduced to his last five dollars. If we remain firm, he'll come to our terms."

Mrs. Brackett spoke confidently, and felt so, but it was not long before she found occasion to reverse her opinion of her brother.

They found him smoking a pipe on the lawn, or grass plat, near the back door.

"Had a pleasant ride?" he asked, lazily.

"Yes, George," said his sister. "What have you been doing?"

"Oh, killing time!" he answered, indifferently. "I have been thinking, Lucinda, that I should have to leave you very soon."

"You mustn't hurry," said Mrs. Brackett; but she felt glad to hear that her brother was likely to leave her soon.

She did not relish having a free boarder, even if he were her own brother, and, besides, judged that they could drive a better bargain with him in that case.

"Oh, I didn't expect to stay here very long," said White. "But I can't go without that hundred dollars."

"Really, George, you can't be aware how hard it is to raise money," said his brother-in-law.

"Oh, yes, I can!" said George, smiling. "I find it deuced uphill work myself," and he glanced knowingly at Mr. Brackett.

"I mean that I find it hard to raise it for you. You see, a hundred dollars is a large sum. If you'd be willing now to take twenty-five and the balance in installments—or, better

still, when we come into our money—I think I
could arrange it."

"My dear brother-in-law," said White, with
a smile, "you do it well—very well, indeed.
If I hadn't been round the world a little, I dare
say I should be taken in, and accept your statement for gospel."

"I hope you don't think my husband would
deceive you, George," said his sister, with
dignity.

"Oh, of course not! Still, I find it is the
general custom to look out for number one."

"You always looked out for number one,
George," said his sister, bluntly.

"Yes I flatter myself I did; but to return
to business. You seem to be at a loss to know
where you can raise the hundred dollars, to
which I am entitled for my services."

"You are right there."

"Then I will tell you where you can find it."

"I wish you would," said Brackett, by no
means prepared for the reply that awaited him.

"It was simple enough, Jeremiah. Draw it
out of the savings bank. You will have four
hundred dollars left."

CHAPTER XLI.

ANDY'S SECRET IS DISCOVERED.

MR. BRACKETT stared at his brother-in-law in
ludicrous dismay, while his wife fairly gasped
for breath.

Here was a revelation, indeed. Their important secret had been discovered, and neither knew what to say.

Mrs. Brackett was the first to recover her wits.

"Who told you we had any money in the savings bank, George?" she demanded.

"Nobody."

"He only guessed it. He doesn't know," she thought. "I can deceive him yet."

"I wish we had money in the bank," she said; "but farming is a poor business. It doesn't pay, and all that Jeremiah and I have been able to do has been to make both ends meet."

"Lucinda, I admire your ready invention— or, shall I say, your ready forgetfulness of facts?" said her brother, with a provoking smile; "but you ought not to try it on me. You must remember that I have been around the world a little; I have a slight knowledge of men, and women, too. You have five hundred dollars in the savings bank, and you know it; and, what's more, I know it."

"Who told you?" demanded his sister, desperately.

A smile passed over her brother's features, as he fixed his eyes on his sister's agitated countenance, and answered, simply:

"I have seen the book."

"Have you dared to go to my bureau drawer?" exclaimed Mrs. Brackett, angrily.

"There it comes out!" said White, laughing. "No, I have not been to your bureau drawer."

"Then, how could you see my bank book?"

"Then it seems you have one, Lucinda. So I thought."

"I have a small account in the bank, I admit," said Mrs. Brackett. "But it's only a few dollars."

"Didn't I tell you I had seen the book? Why do you try to deceive me?"

"Then you have been to my bureau."

"It isn't in your bureau."

"Then where is it? Have you got it with you?"

"No," assured White, unblushingly. "But I know where it is."

"Where is it?" asked his sister, nervously.

"I must tell you the story, and then you will understand how I came to find out about your deposit. That boy of yours, Henry Miller, I distrusted as soon as I saw him. I couldn't place him, but I was convinced I had seen him somewhere, and that his character was bad."

"Just what I always thought!" ejaculated Mrs. Brackett, profoundly gratified at hearing something to Andy's discredit.

"Your instinct was quite correct, my esteemed sister. Well, this afternoon, being left alone in the house, I thought I would search Henry's room, being influenced chiefly by missing a small amount of money a day or two since."

"Did you find it in the boy's room?" asked Lucinda, eagerly.

"No; he was too shrewd to leave money around. The young rascal has a long head, and, I must admit, is unusually smart. I didn't find any money, but on opening the drawer of his dressing table, tucked away in a corner, I saw a savings-bank book. I thought it was his, but on examining it I discovered your name. Of course I opened it, and that is the way I found how much money you had."

"But what could the boy want with the book?" asked Brackett.

"He intended to forge an order and draw some of the money as soon as he went to Jefferson."

"He was to go there to-morrow with father," ejaculated Mrs. Brackett.

"Just so! He's in with the old man, and no wonder. Do you know who he is?"

"I don't know anything beyond his name," said Brackett.

"You don't know that!" said White, triumphantly. "His name is not Henry Miller at all."

"What is it, George?" asked Mrs. Brackett, eagerly.

"Prepare to be astonished. You have been harboring a traitor in your house. His name is Andy Gordon, and his mother is the niece of your father-in-law!"

Mr. and Mrs. Brackett stared at each other in consternation.

CHAPTER XLII.

HOW THE TABLES WERE TURNED.

"OF course," continued White, "it is evident enough why the boy came here. He wanted to worm himself into the confidence of your father-in-law and deprive you of the property which ought to come to you."

"It is shameful!" exclaimed Mr. Brackett, indignantly.

"It's outrageous!" chimed in Mrs. Brackett, furiously.

"You would never have known of this conspiracy but for me, Lucinda," said George White.

"No more we should, George," said his sister.

"And yet you grudge me the small sum you agreed to pay me."

"Jeremiah," said Mrs. Brackett, her parsimony overcome by this consideration, "it is true what George says. We must manage to pay him the money."

"If you think best, Lucindy," said her husband, submissively; "but allow me to suggest that if it is true, and we lose father's money, we shall be very close-pressed ourselves."

"You don't understand, brother-in-law," said White, "that the theft of your bank book will blast Henry's, or rather Andy Gordon's, reputation, and consign him to a prison."

"That will be one comfort," said Mrs. Brackett, her eyes lighting up with malicious exultation.

"Moreover, when the old man finds out what a scamp the boy is, he won't be very apt to make him his heir."

"George, you're a great man," said Brackett, admiringly. "It takes you to find out things."

"Thank you, Jeremiah!" said White, modestly. "You must remember that I have knocked about the world long enough to get my wits sharpened."

"What shall we do about this matter? How shall we proceed? Shall we have the boy arrested?"

"I'll tell you. Send for the old man and the boy at once. Then we'll go upstairs together and discover the bank book in the boy's drawer."

"There's one objection," said Brackett, uneasily. "Father doesn't know that we have any money in the savings bank."

"And you didn't mean that I should know, either, Jeremiah," laughed White. "No matter. Look out for number one. That's my motto, and I can't complain if it's yours also. The old man will have to know now. You can explain the matter some way."

Mr. Brackett went up to Mr. Dodge's room and called him down, while Mrs. Brackett, with a stern frown, summoned Andy from the yard, where he was at work.

When all were gathered in the sitting room, Mrs. Brackett began.

"Father," she said, "we have made an unpleasant discovery."

"What is it?" asked the old man.

"We have discovered that there is a thief in the house."

Curiously it chanced that neither Andy nor Mr. Dodge looked nervous, but each fixed his eyes upon George White.

"Well," said Simon Dodge, after a pause, "who is it?"

"It is that boy !" said Mrs. Brackett, venomously, pointing to Andy.

Andy started, but did not look at all panic-stricken.

"Who charges me with being a thief ?" he demanded, boldly.

"I do !" said George White, smiling triumphantly.

"Oh, it's you, is it ?" said Andy, contemptuously.

"How he brazens it out !" thought Mrs. Brackett.

"Yes," she said, aloud. "My brother has found you out in your evil doings."

"What is Henry charged with stealing ?" asked Mr. Dodge, mildly.

Now it was Mrs. Brackett's turn to look confused.

"Tell him, George," she said.

"My sister's savings-bank book," answered White.

"So you have a deposit in the savings-bank ?" said Simon Dodge, in a tone which rather disconcerted his self-styled daughter-in-law.

"Jeremiah and I, by great economy, had saved something," she explained, hurriedly ; "though we could hardly hope to keep it long, on account of our increasing expenses."

"Suppose we go up to the boy's room, and convince you all of his character," said White.

"Lead on, sir !" said the old man, with dignity. "I shall not believe that Henry is a thief till I have the most convincing proof."

"You shall have the most convincing proof, sir," said George White, pompously.

Together they went upstairs, and filed one by one into the attic chamber occupied by our hero.

George White stepped up to the dressing table already referred to, and opened the drawer wide.

From the corner he drew out the savings-bank book.

"There !" said he, with a flourish, "what do you say to that ?"

"What do you say to it, Henry ?" asked Simon Dodge, kindly.

"That I never saw the book before in my life," answered our hero, promptly.

"What a brazen liar!" ejaculated Mrs. Brackett, holding up both hands in a theatrical manner.

"Then how did it get there, Henry?" asked Brackett, thinking that the question indicated extraordinary sharpness. "It couldn't get into the drawer of its own accord, I take it."

"I agree with you, sir," said Andy, not appearing so much overwhelmed as his questioner expected.

"Then perhaps you'll be kind enough to tell us how it did get there, young man," said George White, magisterially.

"I will, sir," answered Andy, with the utmost coolness. "You put it there."

"I put it there?" exclaimed White, looking around him, with a mocking smile. "My young friend, that is entirely too thin."

"Oh, yes, Henry!" chimed in Mr. Brackett. "You can't make us believe that story, you know."

"I'd like to box your ears, you young slanderer!" exclaimed Mrs. Brackett, glaring at poor Andy, who, however, did not appear to be withered by her glance. "You're a humbug, as well as a thief! You're an impostor, and we've found you out."

"How is Henry an impostor?" asked Mr. Dodge, mildly.

"His name is no more Henry Miller than mine is," vociferated Mr. Brackett, furiously.

"How is that, Henry?" asked Mr. Dodge.

"Mr. Brackett is perfectly right," said our hero.

"Yes," confirmed Simon Dodge; "since you have found it out, I may as well introduce Henry Miller as my grand-nephew, Andy Gordon, of the town of Hamilton."

"What do you say to your grand-nephew turning out to be a thief?" asked Mr. Brackett, triumphantly.

"What do I say? I say that it's a lie!" answered the old man, unexpectedly.

Mr. and Mrs. Brackett stared at each other in dismay.

"He's been detected in the act. The book was found in his drawer."

"And that man put it in," said the old man, with spirit, pointing to George White.

"How dare you say this?" demanded White, angrily.

"Because I have been in the house all the afternoon. I saw you steal into your sister's room and presently emerge with the book. I afterward saw you go up with it to Andy's room. The inference is plain enough."

"I don't believe it," said Mrs. Brackett, faintly.

"Perhaps you will when you hear a little more about this precious brother of yours. Andy, tell Mrs. Brackett what you know about him."

For the first time, George White looked nervous and uneasy. Andy spoke without hesitation:

"The last time I saw him he tried to rob me of a large sum which I was carrying to deposit in the bank, three hundred miles from here. He was in company with an older man, who was caught, and is now serving a term of years in State's prison.

"It's a base lie!" said White, but his face showed that the charge was true. "The boy is accusing me to get off himself. Do you believe this shameful story, Lucinda?"

"Of course I don't. The boy slanders you, George. Will you send for the constable and have the young rascal arrested?"

"As you please, madam," said Andy, coolly. "I shall be able to prove my innocence."

At this moment a loud knocking was heard below, and they hurried downstairs into the sitting room.

"Oh, it's the constable!" said Mrs. Brackett, joyfully. "Mr. Peters, we were just going to send for you to arrest a thief."

"Oh, you've found him out, have you?" asked Mr. Peters, looking rather surprised.

"Do you know anything about it?" said Mrs. Brackett in equal surprise.

"This gentleman gave me full particulars, said Mr. Peters, pointing to his companion, a quiet man in black.

"Who is he?"

"Detective Badger, of New York."

"I see the man I want," said Badger, quietly. "George White, alias Jack Rugg, you are my prisoner!"

"No, it's the boy you are to arrest," said Mrs. Brackett, hurriedly.

"Pardon me, madam," said the detective, "I know my man. Indeed he is well known to the metropolitan police."

White tried to dash by, but unsuccessfully.

The detective brought out a pair of handcuffs, and, with the help of the constable, secured him.

Mrs. Bracket sank into a chair in consternation. She had had no idea of her brother's desperate character, and was unable to utter a word. When the police authorities had carried away their prisoner, Mr. Dodge said to Mr. and Mrs. Brackett :

"After what has occurred, I decline to pass another night under your roof. Andy will go with me to the hotel, and I shall leave you to-morrow, to spend the remainder of my days in his mother's house."

"So this is what you have been plotting, is it?" asked Mrs. Brackett, her eyes flashing. "This is why this boy crept into our home under a false name and under false pretenses!"

"He came because I wrote to his mother, asking her to send him," said Mr. Dodge, with dignity. "He came to help me, and necessarily had to take a new name, in order not to excite your suspicions."

"Your mind has failed," said Mrs. Brackett, sharply, and you have fallen a victim to designing people."

"No, madam. My mind has not failed!" said Simon Dodge. "I have escaped the designs of your

husband and yourself, to whom I have already been
more liberal than you had any right to expect. What
property I have left will go to this boy, who is my
heir, and I recommend you to destroy the forged will,
which you instigated your brother to write. Should
you undertake to interfere with me, this criminal
project of yours shall be revealed to the public.
Come, Andy, go and pack your things. We shall not
spend another night under this roof."

Half an hour later a carriage drew up to the door,
and Andy and the old man drove away, leaving Mr.
and Mrs. Brackett utterly overwhelmed by the discovery of their nefarious plans.

CHAPTER XLIII.
BAD REPORTS ABOUT ANDY.

Mrs. Gordon, in her humble home in Hamliton,
was engaged in sewing toward the close of the afternoon. Her face wore an anxious look, for she had
not heard from Andy for a longer time than usual.
He had written, but the letter had not come to hand.

"I am afraid Andy is sick," she said to herself.
"How long it seems since I last saw him! He is my
all, and if anything should happen to him, I don't
know what would become of me."

Just then in came Miss Susan Peabody, who had
always been attached to Mrs. Gordon.

"Well, Mrs. Gordon, and what do you hear from
Andy?" she asked.

"Nothing," answered the widow, sadly. "I have
not had a letter for nearly a fortnight."

"I heard something to-day that made me very
angry," said Miss Susan.

"About Andy?" asked Mrs. Gordon, looking up.

"Yes, about Andy. It's scandalous!"

"You make me nervous," said the widow. "Tell
me what it is, my good friend."

"As far as I can judge, it's a rumor set afloat by

Herbert Ross, who never liked Andy. He claims to have seen a paragraph—now you mustn't mind it, for of course it's a falsehood—implicating Andy in some crime—stealing, I believe."

"It's a base falsehood!" said Mrs. Gordon, her pale face flushing with justifiable anger.

"Of course it is ; and I wouldn't have spoken of it if the report had not obtained considerable currency. Don't let it trouble you!"

"I won't!" said Mrs. Gordon, with spirit. "It only shows the malice and meanness of the person who set it afloat."

"I suppose one reason for such rumor is, that people are very curious to learn where Andy has gone."

"Very likely. My anxiety is not at all about Andy's behavior, but about his health. If I were only sure that he was well, I would feel perfectly unconcerned."

"That is right, Mrs. Gordon. You look at matters in the right light. I was always very much attached to Andy, as I may some time show. Not many boys would have defended my house and money as bravely as Andy did."

"He was always a good boy. I have never had reason to feel ashamed of him," said the mother, proudly.

Just then there was a knock at the door. Mrs. Gordon rose and opened it. To her surprise she saw before her the tall, dignified figure of Rev. Dr. Euclid, who the reader will remember was the preceptor of the Hamilton Academy.

Mrs. Gordon had a high respect for Dr. Euclid, and welcomed him cordially.

"I am glad to see you, Dr. Euclid," said she. "Won't you come in ?"

"Thank you, Mrs. Gordon; I will come in for five minutes, but I cannot tarry long. When did you hear from your son, Andy ?"

"Not for two weeks—or nearly two weeks."

"He was well?" questioned the doctor.

"Quite well, then; but I am feeling somewhat anxious about him now, on account of the delay of letters."

"Don't let that trouble you. Letters often miscarry."

"I understand," said Mrs. Gordon, "that some malicious person is spreading slanderous reports about Andy. Have you heard anything of the kind, Dr. Euclid?"

"Yes, Mrs. Gordon; but I did not give one moment's credence to them."

"Can you tell me anything about the nature of the reports?"

"It appears that in some paper was published a paragraph touching a certain Andrew Gordon, who was charged with stealing a sum of money from his employer, but it was expressly stated that he was twenty-five years of age. Andy has ill-wishers, however, who, overlooking this circumstance, have been glad to report that he was in trouble."

"It is contemptible!" said Miss Susan Peabody, warmly.

"So it is, my dear Miss Peabody," said Dr. Euclid. "Andy was my favorite pupil, and I will stake my own reputation on his honor and honesty."

"Who is most active in circulating this report?" asked the widow.

"I suspect my pupil, Herbert Ross, who never liked your son, has been active in the matter. He is a selfish, purse-proud idle boy, and Andy is worth half a dozen of him."

"Who is speaking so well of Andy?" asked a young, fresh voice, the sound of which startled all three.

Immediately the door was thrown open, and Andy himself, closely followed by a weak, old man, entered the room.

"Andy, my dear boy!" exclaimed his mother, and folded him with inexpressible joy, in her arms.

"Mother, this is Uncle Simon Dodge," said our hero, when the first greeting was over. "Won't you give him a welcome?"

"Uncle Simon," said Mrs. Gordon, cordially, "I am glad to see you. If you are willing to share our humble home you may consider yourself now at home."

"It is my strongest wish," said the old man, with beaming face.

Here Andy introduced his uncle to Miss Peabody and Dr. Euclid, who gave him a friendly greeting, and expressed a wish to know him better.

"It is well you have come, Andy," said Miss Peabody, "to quiet the reports that are circulating about you."

"What are they?" asked Andy.

"It is said you have stolen a large sum of money, and I presume you are supposed to be in jail."

"Then I'll show myself in the village this evening," said Andy, laughing, "to satisfy my good friends that there's a mistake. Was Herbert Ross very sorry to hear it?"

"I believe he has been one of the most active in spreading the report."

"Poor Herbert! How disappointed he will be!" said Andy, laughing good-naturedly.

CHAPTER XLIV.

CONCLUSION.

AN hour later, Andy met Herbert Ross on the street.

Herbert, who had not heard of our hero's return, started as if he had met a serpent.

"Good-evening, Herbert," said Andy, good-naturedly.

"Have you got back?" asked Herbert, curiosity struggling with disappointment.

"It looks like it, doesn't it?"

"I thought you had got into trouble?" said Herbert. "How did you manage to get out of it?"

Andy laughed.

"I hear," he said, "that some of my good friends have been circulating bad reports about me. It's a pity to spoil their enjoyment, but it's another person entirely who has misbehaved himself. As I am not twenty-five, I don't see how anyone should think it was I."

"That might be a mistake, you know. The name was Andrew Gordon."

"Then I wish Andrew Gordon would change his name. I assure you, Herbert, I have no intention of taking up the business of stealing."

"You'd better not," said Herbert, stiffly, feeling rather suspicious that Andy was laughing at him.

"Did you make any money when you were away?" asked Herbert.

"Oh, yes! I got a situation directly."

"Was the pay good?"

"Fifty cents a week and my board," answered Andy, gravely.

Herbert sniffed scornfully.

"You'd better have stayed at home," he said.

"I don't know about that. I am well satisfied with the success of my journey."

"You can't be janitor again!" said Herbert, triumphantly.

"Why not?"

"Another boy got it, and Dr. Euclid won't put him out, just to oblige you."

"I am not a candidate for the position of janitor," said Andy.

"Don't you mean to go to school, then?"

"Oh, yes! I want to continue my education," said Andy.

"You know enough already for a poor boy."

"Thank you for the compliment!"

"You'd better get a place somewhere to work."

" Thank you ! But, as I propose to go to college, I shall go back to the academy."

" Go to college ! How can you go to college ? Why, you haven't a cent !"

" I can't stop to explain, Herbert. But you'll hear before long."

Herbert did hear, and so did the whole village, that Andy had brought back with him a rich uncle, who was credited with being worth fifty thousand dollars.

We know that this is not true, but rumor is prone to exaggerate the extent of a man's fortune.

It was, moreover, reported—and this on good authority—that Andy was to be his uncle's heir.

It is surprising how much his social importance, and that of his mother, were enhanced by this fact. Even those who had credited the story of Andy's being a thief were among the first to congratulate him ; and Herbert Ross, disagreeable as the news was to him, gave up his sneers and became actually civil. Indeed, he would have become intimate with Andy, if our hero had encouraged him to be so.

The little cottage proved too small and inconvenient, now that the widow had another inmate, and Mr. Dodge bought a handsome house opposite that of Lawyer Ross, from a manufacturer about to leave town, and with it the furniture, both of which he got at an excellent bargain.

Andy went back to school, and soon made up what he had lost by absence. He was no longer janitor, but he was never ashamed to speak of the time in which he had filled that office.

It never rains but it pours. When the Misses Peabody died it turned out that they left their entire property to Andy, having no near relatives to bequeath it to.

He is recognized as the heir of Mr. Dodge, who is still living in comfortable enjoyment of life at the age of eighty, and so our young hero is likely to have no pecuniary anxieties.

As I write, he is a member of the senior class at Yale College, and holds a distinguished rank among his class-mates.

Herbert Ross is in the same class, but he drags along near the foot, and seems likely to confer little credit upon his *alma mater*.

Andy will study law, and we may fairly expect a credible, perhaps brilliant, position for the young man whose early poverty compelled him to fill the position of a janitor.

A few words about some of our subordinate characters and our story ends.

Mr. and Mrs. Brackett were terribly mortified by the disastrous issue of their unlawful designs. They understood that they had overreached themselves, and they will always remain discontented and unhappy.

It leaked out in their town that Mrs. Brackett's brother was confined in State's prison for burglary, and this was by no means agreeable. George White would not receive a very cordial welcome now at the farm.

Joshua Starr was found dead one day in his barn. The property which he had accumulated by miserly ways and unscrupulous dealings, went to a cousin whom he hated. Was his life worth living?

Mike Hogan and George White are still boarding in a State institution, where they are likely to remain till the end of their term, though they would willingly relieve the State of the burden of their maintenance.

Rev. Dr. Euclid, honored and respected as of old, still remains principal of Hamilton Academy. He follows with strong interest the career of Andy Gordon, the greatest favorite among the hundreds of pupils whom he has had under his instruction, and he confidently predicts for him a brilliant future. May his prediction be fulfilled.

THE END.